THE TROLL-HUMAN WAR

THE TROLL WARS TRILOGY: BOOK TWO

LEAH R CUTTER

KNOTTED ROAD PRESS

The Troll-Human War
The Troll Wars Trilogy: Book Two
Copyright © 2019 Leah Cutter
All rights reserved
Published by Knotted Road Press
www.KnottedRoadPress.com

ISBN: 978-1-64470-041-9

Cover Art:
ID 25947799 © Prometeus | Depositphoto.com

Cover and interior design copyright © 2019 Knotted Road Press
http://www.KnottedRoadPress.com

Come someplace new…
If you'd like to be notified of new releases, sign up for my newsletter.

I will never spam you or use your email for nefarious purposes. You can also unsubscribe at any time.

http://www.LeahCutter.com/newsletter/

Seattle Trolls

The Changeling Troll

The Princess Troll

The Fairy-Bridge Troll

The Troll-Demon War

The Troll-Human War

The Troll-Troll War

The Cassie Stories

Poisoned Pearls

Tainted Waters

Spoiled Harvest

Bloodied Ice

Tanish Empire Trilogy

The Glass Magician

The Desert Heart

The Ghost Dog

The Shadow Wars Trilogy

The Raven and the Dancing Tiger

The Guardian Hound

War Among the Crocodiles

The Clockwork Fairy Kingdom

The Clockwork Fairy Kingdom

The Maker, the Teacher, and the Monster

The Dwarven Wars

The Chronicles of Franklin

Franklin Versus The Popcorn Thief

Franklin Versus The Soul Thief

Franklin Versus The Child Thief

Contemporary Fantasy

Siren's Call

The Immortals' War

Circle of Air

CHAPTER ONE

CHRISTINE ROARED HER DISPLEASURE AS SHE SWUNG her great ax over her head, bringing it down hard and dispatching yet another damned demon. The group she fought this time were like huge corrupted lions, with sickly yellow slitted eyes, ugly snouts pushed out from a flat face with wickedly sharp upper and lower fangs, and a tawny, scraggly hide that wouldn't even make good leather. Their powerful rear legs enabled them to make long leaps. They frequently ran away from the battle only to come barreling back in and surprising the unaware.

Christine had lost more than one of the rowdy boys learning that trick.

The two groups—about forty souls on a side—fought on a dry savannah, the grass long since grown brittle. The smell of the desiccated ground swirled up around Christine every time she took a step. A brown dusty haze filled the air, making it difficult to breathe. Though the sky appeared gray and covered with clouds, the unseen sun still overheated the place.

Trolls didn't really sweat, but even Christine felt her pores opening up in this sauna. Her muscled, olive-colored arms glistened even in the dim light. The haft of her double-headed ax felt solid against her meaty hands, big enough around that she didn't have to worry about her long claws digging into her palms. She hadn't bit one of her opponents, tearing out their throat with her long tusks. Not yet. Mainly because the smell of the demons was so foul she couldn't imagine getting it closer to her face.

She might, though. These bastards were really pissing her off.

The plane they fought on was *exactly* the wrong place for the Risilodan—the rowdy boys who still battled—to be in. While they'd diligently stuck with her, following the fight from the previous plane to this one, they were flagging.

Christine had never bluntly asked the rowdy boys about their heritage, but she'd always suspected that they had frost giants as ancestors, given their height. Christine was tall for a troll—nearly eight feet tall—but some of the rowdy boys were at least fourteen feet tall. They had pasty white faces, no tusks, and huge noses. Their magic was mostly frost and ice based, which wasn't doing them any good here. There was no moisture to suck out of the air, no hidden rivers to bring up out of the ground.

Still, they grimly fought on with their huge spiked clubs that were eight feet long and were often reinforced with a metal bar in the middle of them.

The next demon in front of Christine reared up on its hind legs, intending to slash at her. Its snapping jaw missed her shoulder by mere inches. She choked up on her ax and struck the thing in its neck as it was dropping back to the ground, the damned blood spraying everywhere.

She was never going to get the smell of gore and blood out of her armor. She'd grown to appreciate the need for a dress uniform as well as a fighting one. She wore something similar to the king's guard: a heavy, blue-dyed vest with solid metal rings sewn to it; typical troll breaches made out of a brown wool cloth that she'd enchanted to be as tough as metal-reinforced armor, that ended just below her knee; tall black leather boots designed for her troll feet that were surprisingly comfortable; and a peaked helmet that rested high across her forehead and sides, gold plated so that her warriors could easily distinguish her from the other guards who all had silver helmets.

That gold helmet also marked her as important, so she got a lot more attention from the enemy as well.

That was fine by her. Her human brother didn't call her a "badass warrior princess" for nothing. She'd been training for this for the last five years, sparring with the king's guard as well as Patrick the orc several times a week.

Yet, none of her training could have prepared her for the grueling reality of war.

Lars and the demons had started the Great War six weeks before. Demons had poured into hundreds of the settled worlds, decimating the *kith and kin*. They wouldn't accept any terms. No one was allowed to surrender or switch sides and suddenly align themselves with the demons. Not yet. Christine's generals had surmised that at some point the demons would start offering deals, thereby turning the tide of the war further.

Christine had been raised by a human family, a changeling, unaware that she was actually a troll until she'd broken the spell hiding the truth. She understood now why some of her generals had considered her soft.

Not until she'd been in battles, day in and day out, death her one constant companion, had she understood what "soft" meant. And how she couldn't afford to be, not any longer.

Plus, they were losing. She met with her generals every night, and while no one had actually bluntly stated the truth, everyone knew it. It was just a matter of time before the demons poured into the human plane and declared themselves the victors of the Great War. They were already planning their assault. The Host would fight on the behalf of the humans—the angels, white elves, and other beings of light.

But they'd lose, because the *kith and kin*, and all the other races that weren't human, were going to be long since vanquished, or allied with the demons. The humans would be slaughtered by the billions.

Fortunately, demons were easy to bribe, so the *kith and kin* had learned early on about the best weapon that the demons had—something called a corruption crystal. Each crystal was tiny, no bigger than the nailbed on Christine's pinky finger. They looked like enchanted rock crystals, clear or white with a pale glow.

By itself, a single crystal slowly eroded the magic and moral fiber of any being they were placed next to. Over the last four weeks, the magicians had come to realize that the effect was cumulative. The longer a being was in the proximity of a corruption crystal, the more hopeless they became.

In larger quantities, like say, if every demon in an army carried a corruption crystal, the overall effect was to severely weaken the magical attacks of whatever army the demons attacked.

Christine and her generals had figured out magical spells to determine which groups of combatants had the crystals and which didn't, choosing to fight the unaided groups whenever they could.

It was one of their luckier breaks—demons weren't necessarily organized. Several of their troops either hadn't been issued the crystals, or more likely, had refused to carry them due to some sort of demonic family squabbling or power plays.

The unaided demons fought back by plane hopping. They'd leave whatever plane of existence they were on and hop to a new world where there might be reinforcements, or they'd choose a field of battle where they had an advantage.

Like now.

If Christine led the rowdy boys to a different plane, there was no guarantee the demons would come after them. "Follow through" was yet another thing that demons weren't known for.

She roared her approval when she saw that a group of the rowdy boys had finally managed to find some water—maybe they'd used their own rations of it—and had conjured a puddle big enough that they could shape ice daggers from it.

It was one of the reasons why the rowdy boys made

such effective fighters in these battles. Demons primarily fought with fire or acid, not ice. They could frequently be vanquished using cold spells.

The head of the rowdy boys—Albrecto—accurately threw the ice daggers at the enemy, killing one by stabbing it in the eyes, a second in the chest, and a third right down its open mouth.

Christine cheered. So did the rowdy boys.

They might win this skirmish yet.

Every little bit helped.

A foul wind carried the scent of burning flesh. Hot ash flew across the dried field.

Another portal opened up.

Christine gulped.

A massive group of demons raced out of the gaping black hole that had just appeared.

The ice daggers shriveled in Albrecto's hands.

The new group were armed with the corruption crystals.

Instead of being evenly matched, her side was now outnumbered three to one.

Though Christine knew the rowdy boys wouldn't like it, she still sounded the call.

"Retreat! Retreat!"

Albrecto turned toward her, probably getting ready to argue.

Christine didn't get to hear a word of it, however.

A flying disc came whizzing by.

It took Albrecto's head off.

"Retreat!" Christine called again, quickly shaping a broad portal to get them the hell out of there. She couldn't make it tall enough for the rowdy boys to get through without stooping. She'd have to apologize later.

Hopefully, the demons wouldn't bother following.

Or if they did, well, they were in for a surprise of their own.

Her troops started trickling through the gate. Christine defended their backs as well as she could. She called on her air element to knock away the damned discs that came flying toward them. As her group retreated, behind them, she started a raging fire.

Earlier in the war, she'd been too concerned about possibly doing damage on whatever world she'd ended up fighting on.

Now, she was much, *much* more concerned about getting her people out alive.

And while the demons might have an affinity toward fire, her own fire element was too angry for them to just pass through.

As far as Christine could tell, she only lost one more rowdy boy before they'd all vanished into the portal.

Only after her people were safe did Christine go through the portal herself.

She could already hear Ozlandia, the head of the king's guard, yelling at her for putting herself in such danger.

Too bad.

Christine might be an actual princess, heir to the throne of Trollville, but she still had to do the right thing.

She backed her way through the portal, shutting it as she went through. Yet another dangerous thing to do, as she could get herself trapped between the planes.

She made it, though, back to the human plane. The rowdy boys looked around them, astonished.

Christine couldn't help but laugh. The sound grated on her ears. It had been weeks, probably, since she'd laughed.

But the expression on the faces of the rowdy boys was too much.

While it was the middle of summer in Seattle, she'd landed them high up on Mount Rainier, where the ground was still covered in snow.

When traveling through a portal, a being normally could only go someplace that they'd been to before. While Christine had never been to this location before, her air element had, and had shared enough images of this place that she'd been able to go there in her time of need.

"Thank you," said Constenllo, Albrecto's second in command. "The wounded are already being tended to."

That was why Christine had brought them directly to a place filled with ice and snow. She had already started shivering in the cold, but it was what the rowdy boys needed.

"No, thank you," Christine said. "For trusting me. For following me. For fighting."

Constenllo shrugged. "It's still just a game for most of them," he said softly. "We've lost some of us. It won't be serious until half of us are gone. Then, well, we may just have to tend to our own."

Christine nodded. She'd heard the same sentiment from other groups she'd fought with. They'd had some losses, suffered a bit. If the war continued, they may have to rethink their alliances.

Christine had to stop the war. Win it, somehow.

She just had no idea how.

Back in her own home, deep underground on the human side of the fairy bridge, Christine soaked her aching muscles in her tub. Her water and fire elementals worked together to keep the water warm enough, as well as make it swirl and bubble around her.

The tub was actually a huge human jacuzzi tub that she'd bought online. With her earth powers, Christine had dug a pit large enough to slide the tub into, placing the lip of it even with the ground. She had no electricity down here, no running water, either, so everything else had to be done with magic, like filling the tub, heating the water, and making it swirl.

Christine had spent some time fixing up her tub room. It was one of two rooms where she'd actually tiled the floor instead of just having good packed dirt. (The other being her kitchen floor. While it was possible to use magic to wipe up spilled food, it was easier in the long run to just sweep it up by hand.) She'd chosen large, square, Spanish-style red tiles for the floor in here, with smaller, pretty, hand-painted tiles around the lip of the tub. Sometimes she'd keep the water warm and the tiles cool, then she'd lean back against the side of the tub and stretch her arms out, the contrast deliciously decadent.

That evening, Christine kept all her body under the water. Despite how she'd trained, she still got sore after so much exertion. She'd grown measurably stronger over the last few weeks of fighting, however.

In the privacy of her own thoughts, Christine had to admit that the fighting had been exciting at first—the rush of battle, the exhilaration of slaying demons.

The thrill had worn off quickly.

Her attention had turned more and more to how to prevent battles (impossible with the demons randomly attacking), surviving battles (more difficult now as the demons killed more good troops), as well as winning the war.

No one had been able to come up with a good defense for the corruption crystals yet. Part of the problem was how difficult it was to study them. Their influence corrupted even the strongest magician. They couldn't be held in a single location for long. And no one had figured out how to neutralize them either. Any sort of magical sphere wrapped around them became corrupted over time.

Combatting the corruption crystals was key.

Christine had to admit that the other key was figuring out how to neutralize Lars Sorgenfreys. He'd been imprisoned for five years, in part because of her.

However, he'd used that time well.

Demons were impulsive. That was part of their nature. They didn't plan.

Lars had spent his time in prison actually devising a plan for how to win the Great War. It was one of the things that her generals all agreed on. Demons hated losing more than anything else. Fear of failure had been one of the things that had kept them in check for all the centuries leading up to this war.

Now, they thought they had a real chance of winning due to Lars' plan.

And they might yet, if Christine didn't figure out how to stop Lars.

Christine had studied demons in detail over the last five years, before the war. (And really, was her life now going to be divided between Before the War and After the War? When previously it had been before she'd broken the changeling spell and after?)

Minor demons tended to be more similar one to another, like the last race she'd just fought. The upper level demons, the ones who were members of the important demon families, tended to be individual and rarely looked alike. It was as though their parents chose the characteristics they wanted for their offspring, putting together an amalgamation of wings, fangs, claws, attack, etc.

Lars had bone-like struts that made up his wings, with black, tattered, leather-like material stretched between them. They looked horrifying, and he towered over Christine when they were fully expanded, but they weren't very useful. He couldn't fly with them, and she'd been able to catch them with her winds and knock him off balance. He had sickly looking yellow scales that covered his chest, while black and white scales covered most of the rest of his body. Those were good protection for him, as both her ax as well as her magic tended to bounce right off.

He spat an icky black acid that had ruined her metal-and-magic enhanced cloak the last time she'd fought him. He also had the usual talons at the ends of his fingers and toes, plus a wicked tail.

If she thought about it, he was sort of like a corrupted dragon. But instead of a lust for gold, he had a lust for power.

If he won the Great War, he'd have all the power he wanted. For centuries.

How long did a demon normally live? No one seemed to know. (Because of course, no one bothered writing down these sorts of things or keeping accurate histories. It was one of her serious grievances with the *kith and kin*.) Trolls lived between one hundred and fifty to two hundred years. Many of the *kith and kin* races were long lived as well.

So how could Christine stop Lars? She didn't have to kill him but merely discredit him. Maybe even trick the demons into thinking they were losing the war.

While Christine had learned how to be sneaky because she'd been raised as a human, most trolls didn't have that level of guile.

Humans were the sneakiest of all the races, after the demons.

Unfortunately, humans were the most vulnerable to the corruption crystals.

Christine felt as though she constantly fought battles on two fronts: one with the demons, and the other with the humans, to keep them from getting completely corrupted and turning against the *kith and kin*, those who were trying to protect them.

And Christine was growing tired, herself. Discouraged. It wasn't because of some damned magical crystal, but due to the reality of the situation.

Tomorrow would bring more battle. More killing. More death.

She had to get off this treadmill without getting herself killed or losing the war. She had to get ahead of Lars somehow.

She just wished she knew how.

CHAPTER TWO

LARS SAT BEHIND HIS BIG DESK IN HIS OFFICE FACING three of his generals, the ones responsible for the latest defeat. The office was on the human plane. Lars wore his human guise, bad-boy blond hair falling over his forehead, ice-cold blue eyes, sharp nose and noble chin. His massive desk held important folders and reports, not that he'd actually bothered to read them—he had minions who read them and summed them into bullet points for him. But they looked important.

Maps covered the walls, most of them now gloriously covered in red, where the demons had attacked and won. Lars had a few trophies hanging up as well, heads of various *kith and kin* races that the demons had wiped out.

The place of honor just behind him was still empty. That spot was reserved for that damned princess troll, Christine.

Lars had plans for her. A trap that he'd spring. Soon.

His chair floated half an inch off the floor. No one could see that, however. He kept the fact that he never actually set foot on the human plane hidden from most of the demons: they wouldn't understand that he was being hunted, and that if he set one foot on the ground he'd be captured and imprisoned again. No, if the demons realized that Lars floated above the earth, they'd think he was weak.

Then again, over the last few weeks, Lars had come to appreciate that most demons were, in fact, stupid.

Like the three generals standing in front of his desk.

Lars had given them human names, explaining that it was impossible for his human throat to pronounce Xmghre'klpghyop and the other names accurately.

He didn't bother explaining the significance of Larry, Moe, and Curly, the three stooges.

Larry appeared to be the brightest of the three, though that wasn't saying much. He was related to the horse-faced demons who generally did menial labor, like the two guards who'd watched Lars when he'd been in prison. Larry had risen so high in rank because he actually had some talent, as he didn't have the proper family connections to smooth out those sorts of things for him.

Out of respect for Lars, all three demons had shrunk down to be merely tall humans instead of towering demons. So while Larry would normally be twelve or fourteen feet tall, he was just over six feet tall. His skin was bright red. Lars would bet that he oiled it just for this occasion, so that it glistened. Larry's head was in the shape of a horse, while his body was that of a muscular human, with four arms. Lars had seen Larry in battle. Lars had to admit that Larry had some moves.

Moe was the shortest of the three, pudgy and soft

looking. Pimples, warts, and boils covered his head and chest, the one on his left cheek nearly the size of his nose, with three long hairs growing out of it. Lars couldn't imagine how Moe's wife endured looking at such a face; however, Moe had supposedly fathered over a dozen offspring. His skin was a pasty gray color and kept flaking off whenever Moe scratched himself, which was far too often for Lars' taste. (He was going to have to use a serious cleaning spell when these three left.)

Curly was bald, of course. She had spiked wings with red feathers that she kept politely folded against her back, a long snout with wicked fangs, and glowing golden eyes. The scales that covered her face and back were a polluted white color. Her belly was a dull blue. A short tail dropped gracefully from the end of her spine, armed with sharpened gray-metal spikes.

Lars might have found Curly attractive, that was, until she opened her mouth. In battle, she spewed an icy miasma, very unusual for a demon. In conversation, she had an incredibly nasal tone that was worse than human laughter, making Lars feel as though three inch nails were being drilled into his spine.

He really hadn't wanted to bring her into his office and have a conversation with her. Or the others. But the three of them really needed to be called on the carpet at this point, as it were.

"So, can one of you explain to me what the hell you thought you were doing by going and attacking the Sonicasmer?"

They were one of the races of the *kith and kin*. They had practically no magical abilities, and instead were ferocious physical fighters, despite the fact that the tallest of them barely reached three feet tall. They looked like hedgehogs, covered in blue fur with a small snout filled with sharp teeth. They were fiercely competitive, and downright vicious when cornered.

Larry spoke up. "Well, someone suggested that since they were just the next plane over, and we'd finished cleaning up the Jungalonions early, that we might as well just go and strike there next."

Lars rolled his eyes. "Did you think you could just go and attack the Sonicasmer? That they'd roll over and die easily?"

The three generals all shuffled their feet, almost in unison, as if it were a dance that they'd practiced together.

"The boys needed to let off some steam," Moe said. "The Sonicasmer should have been a soft target."

"Why would you ever think that the Sonicasmer would be easy?" Lars asked, honestly confused.

The three of them shuffled their feet again.

Really, was he going to have to break out some dance music for them?

"There may have been a bet involved," Larry finally admitted.

Moe looked down, scratching at the back of his neck, before he then ran the nails across his teeth, collecting and eating whatever it was that had been trapped there.

Ewww.

"And possibly some alcohol," Curly added after a few moments.

Damn. Maybe Lars should get a recording of that voice to use it as a new torture device for humans. He made himself take a deep breath, trying to settle his shoulders back down.

"I want you to realize it isn't so much that you lost that's the problem," Lars said. These three needed to understand the full implications of their actions. "You didn't follow the plan."

The three generals looked at each other, then shrugged. "We was going to get to them later, though, right?" Larry asked. "They're on the list."

Lars couldn't contain his sigh. "No, you idiot. They are *not* on the list of those who are going to be attacked."

Moe blinked bleary eyes at Lars as he picked his nose thoughtfully. "I coulda sworn, boss, that they was on a list."

"Yes," Lars said. He shook his head. This was the problem with trying to keep his generals and commanders informed of his plans. They'd go ahead and make stupid mistakes like this. "They were on the list of *kith and kin* to be turned into *allies* later."

"Oh," the three generals said in unison.

At least the other two voices masked some of the nail-driving aspects of Curly's voice.

"Maybe we could still turn them," Larry said optimistically.

"No, we can't. You three fucked up any chance of that by killing off most of their king's children, yet *failing* to kill the king himself." Lars let more anger creep into his voice. "What you've done is to drive the Sonicasmer, who as you will all admit are fearsome fighters, into the arms of the enemy. If you'd bothered to follow *the plan*, we could have swept them up as allies. Now, we're going to have to fight them. Again."

"Sorry, boss."

"Sorry."

"Sorry."

Lars growled at them, still pissed off. "Now, you three are some of my best generals. Do you think you could find it within yourselves to actually do what you're told next time?"

Larry and the others visibly relaxed. "Of course, boss," Larry said easily. "We can do that."

Lars didn't like the casual tone Larry used.

"Good," Lars said. "Now, you need to go and report to Misalmorth."

Huh. He hadn't realized that a bright red, horse-headed demon could grow that pale. Almost pastel colored.

"Who?" Moe asked, glancing between his two compatriots.

"The head of reporting," Larry said through gritted teeth, as though he was trying to maintain some sort of pleasant expression on his face.

Both Moe and Curly gulped.

"Once you've actually read through and compiled all the reports currently on Misalmorth's desk, you can return to active duty," Lars purred.

"Yes, boss," Larry said, nodding. He glanced over at the other two and gave them a curt nod.

"Yes, boss," Moe and Curly both responded.

Interesting. The three of them had formed an alliance,

as Lars had suspected. Were they thinking that they could overthrow Lars at some critical moment?

Probably.

And if Lars were an ordinary demon, they might be able to.

But Lars was different. Extraordinary.

He had plans. As they would all learn soon enough.

If he could just get the other demons to follow them…

"Dismissed," Lars said sharply.

The three of them looked around, as if surprised that was it.

Lars rolled his eyes. On the one bare wall of the office, a portal suddenly appeared.

"Thanks, boss!" Curly chirped as she tromped through the opening, the others following.

Lars took a deep sigh, then immediately regretted it, as Moe seemed to have released all the gas that had been trapped inside him as he left. A quick human cleansing spell took care of that before Lars' eyes started watering and he started choking and coughing.

He'd have to watch those three. That they'd shown some initiative going after the Sonicasmer was actually a good thing. He needed generals who could think for themselves.

However, he couldn't give them too long of a leash, or they'd turn and bite him.

Lars turned his thoughts to the Sonicasmer. Was it possible to twist this to his advantage? Or had he just handed his enemy one more plum?

He floated and thought, going deep inside himself, to an introspective place that few demons had ever reached.

When he came out, he still didn't have a plan for the Sonicasmer. But he'd watch and see if maybe they could be incorporated later, possibly into his final trap for Christine.

Plans within plans. Wheels in wheels.

CHAPTER THREE

"But I don't want to move back in with my parents!" Tina complained. "You, of all beings, should understand that."

"I do," Christine said, nodding. "But you're not doing very well on your own."

"Am too," Tina said. She realized that their postures mirrored one another identically, chin stuck out stubbornly, arms crossed over chest, legs in a wide stance.

But that was where the similarities ended, today. Tina had blonde hair and blue eyes and was full of light. Or at least, she used to be. Christine's human face still bore a superficial resemblance to Tina's, with the same nose, thin lips, and round cheeks. However, Christine had a hard edge to her now, her eyes lit with a fire that Tina could only long for.

Christine sighed and used her right hand to indicate Tina's bedroom, where they both stood. "You're not doing that well. Look at this place. Really look at it, if you can."

"All right, so it's a little messy," Tina admitted.

Christine cocked a single eyebrow at her.

"Fine. So maybe it's a lot messy. What's that got to do with anything?" Tina asked. Sure, there were books piled everywhere. Christine could appreciate that, right?

But maybe Christine was complaining about the dirty dishes stacked on the floor next to the bed. And the sheets that, okay, could really use washing. Or the piles of both clean clothes that Tina couldn't be bothered putting away, as well as the all the dirty ones strewn across the carpet.

Christine waved her hand again, indicating Tina herself. She looked down. "Fine. I should probably change this shirt." She'd slept in it one, no, maybe three nights. A long white streak of toothpaste went down one side, though it wasn't that noticeable as the shirt had been white at one point. Now, it seemed a yellowish gray. Why was that?

Tina took a deep breath. Wow, that was rank. Was that her? Tina pinched the front of her shirt and brought it up to her nose. Yup. She needed a shower.

What was wrong with her?

For a moment, the desolation of Tina's room hit her. It was a mess. *She* was a mess. She didn't used to be like this. She remembered when there had been light and air in her room. The shades were all drawn, and given the piles of dishes and junk sitting on the window sill, she hadn't raised them in a while. The windows themselves were locked tight. She remembered doing that now, as if in a dream, locking and hiding herself away.

"What's happening to me?" Tina asked Christine.

"You're not doing well here," Christine said. "We need to move you."

"I can clean it up," Tina said. "I can take better care of myself. I promise," she said.

The thought of leaving her apartment, of going outside, terrified her.

"It's nice and sunny out," Christine promised. "No rain."

"Ugh, it's too hot," Tina countered immediately. The news—she'd watched the news recently, right? Mainly because it was all so bad and depressing and it fit her mood. "We've been having such a heatwave. Maybe we could wait until the weekend when it's cooler."

"No," Christine said. "Because by then, you'll have come up with another excuse. And another. And another. I need to get you out of here. Now."

"What if I don't want to?" Tina said. "I'll just turn around and leave and come back here no matter where you take me," she warned.

"We've talked about this," Christine said slowly.

Had they? Tina couldn't remember.

"It's why you're going to your parents' house. So that you'll be protected," Christine said.

"Imprisoned," Tina said. "You know how they'll treat me. They'll lock me up."

"You've already done that to yourself," Christine pointed out.

Tina opened her mouth to protest, but then closed it again without saying anything.

She was in her own townhouse. And she had done it to herself. "But why?" Tina asked. "Why can't I take care of myself?"

"Because you're sick," Christine told her. "And I'm

going to take you someplace where you can hopefully get better."

"Fine," Tina said, suddenly angry. She'd show Christine, this troll, just what she was made out of.

Tina readied herself to escape, to run. Even though the thought of leaving her room terrified her, being taken away and locked up someplace else scared her more.

However, Christine didn't open the door. Instead, she sketched a portal immediately in front of it.

"How did you do that?" Tina asked. She felt her eyes bugging out of her face. "I can't do any magic in this room. No one can."

Christine gave Tina brittle laugh. It went along with the hard shell that Christine now wore. "Only half of that statement is true. You can't do magic in this room. But," Christine paused for a moment, making Tina look at her closely, "I'm going to take you to someplace where you may be able to get your magic back."

"Really?" Tina asked, taking a step forward, toward the open portal. "You can get my magic back? You promise?"

Christine shook her head. "I cannot guarantee that you'll get all your magic back," she said honestly.

Tina rolled her eyes. Of course, Christine wouldn't lie to her. Or make a promise that she might not be able to keep.

"Then why should I go?" Tina asked. "If I can't have my magic?" It was one of the things that had kept her paralyzed in her room.

If her magic was truly gone, what was there left for her?

The darkest parts of her soul had even started talking

about how it might be better for everyone if Tina was just…no longer there. Since her magic had left. Why shouldn't she just depart as well?

Facing that fear…being mundane…no. It was much better to just stay here.

Christine seemed to realize just how close Tina stood to the edge of that precipice.

"I cannot promise that you'll get your magic back at this place," Christine said. "What I will promise is that I will stick with you, that we will keep trying. If this doesn't work, we'll try something else. I won't give up on you. I promise."

Tina shivered at the words. Though she couldn't hear the bell-like tones that accompanied them, not like she once could when she'd had magic, she still felt them, somehow, at the core of her soul.

When a troll, and in particular, a royal troll like Christine, made a promise, they were bound to keep it. Records of those vows were held deep in the earth and could be called up by the Host as well as others.

Tina felt herself deflate.

While she now knew that Christine wouldn't give up on her, she knew that she'd already given up on herself.

But Tina could play along. For now.

"Let's go then," Tina said, pasting a bright smile on her face. It hurt to make that expression. Had it been that long since she'd smiled?

"Good," Christine said, sounding relieved.

Tina glanced around her room. "What should I take with me?"

"Nothing," Christine said. "Leave it. Someone that your parents have hired will come in and clean."

"What if I don't want them touching my stuff?" Tina huffed.

"They won't hurt anything," Christine assured her. "They'll just straighten it all up. So it will be nice when you return."

Tina nodded, acknowledging that Christine had just played the exact right card, by giving her the hope that she might be able to come back to her townhouse.

"I just—I need my wand," Tina said.

Christine shook her head. "Not until we make sure that it hasn't been corrupted."

"What do you mean?" Tina asked. "I haven't corrupted my wand! I don't do dark magic!"

"I know," Christine said patiently. "We've talked about this before, remember?"

Tina shook her head warily. "You're just trying to make me weaker," she accused Christine.

"Look, your parents are going to get you a new wand," Christine said. "So that you'll be able to start practicing magic again as soon as possible."

"Really?" Tina asked. "I miss being able to do magic," she confessed.

"I know," Christine said. "So let's go and see if we can get you practicing again."

"All right," Tina said. She took another step toward the door. "You'll be there, right?"

"When I can," Christine said.

"But—"

"I've got a war to fight," Christine growled. "A war that you're supposed to help me win. Remember?"

Tina remembered now, how she'd once had a Destiny.

Until Christine had stolen it.

"Fine," Tina said. She marched right through the portal without another word.

She was going to get her magic back. Somehow.

Then she was going after Christine, and getting her Destiny back.

CHAPTER FOUR

Nikolai was waiting on a group of ogres when Christine came through the portal into the shop.

He hadn't seen her in a few weeks. Before the war, Christine worked in the shop once a week. Never waiting on customers, of course. She was a troll. Customer service wasn't natural to her. Instead, she inventoried the items in his huge collection of boxes that he'd bought at various estate sales over the decades.

Christine stood for a moment and took a deep breath, visibly relaxing.

Nik could understand. All Christine had been doing was fighting. He was glad that she'd come to see him as a little bit of normalcy would do her good, as well remind her of what exactly she was fighting for.

Not that Nik's Emporium and Trade Goods was necessarily "normal."

The nature of the posters covering the upper portion of the eighteen-foot tall walls had changed over the past few weeks. Instead of advertising vitality ointments and hair growth incantations, now they showed ads for healing potions and invisibility charms, as well as formulas for protecting food so that it would last for years.

All indications of the war and how badly it was going.

Wooden shelves lined the wide open floor. He'd built many of them, enchanting them over the centuries so that the wood wouldn't age.

He used the same spells on himself, his own wooden body. He couldn't replace a part that wore out, or he would have gradually replaced all of himself, grown into a taller version.

He'd come to accept that he'd spend an eternity being just three feet tall. That was all the bigger of a wooden body that he'd been able to create given the technology of the time, over two thousand years before, when he'd had an angel transfer his consciousness from his human body into the wooden one.

Strange. Since the start of the Great War, he'd come to miss his soul a lot more. He wasn't sure why.

Christine carefully avoided looking at the ogres as she slipped behind the counter and into the backroom. They were one of the groups of the *kith and kin* who had originally aligned with the demons in the war.

But Nik was committed to staying neutral during this war, as he had been during the last Great War, which had occurred over two thousand years before. It was part of his pledge, a promise that he'd made to the angel in exchange for helping him slide into his wooden body.

The promise had never chaffed so much before, either.

Then again, Nik had never had an assistant like

Christine before. Someone who was important to the war effort, on the side that he privately wanted to win.

He could work with demons, with humans, with the Host as well as the *kith and kin*. His preference was still the humans, though.

When the ogres had finished their business, buying simple components for portal and healing spells, Nik was able to slip into the backroom.

Industrial metal shelves lined the walls of the small room, though only a quarter of them held boxes. An open box sat on the low table that Nik had brought in. He wasn't as thorough as Christine when it came to creating an inventory. She'd been a librarian before she'd broken the changeling spell, and was all about taxonomies and information systems.

But she'd set up a good system for him, and he tried to follow it when he could.

"Hey, Nik," Christine said as he came through the curtain. Her attention was on one of the items on the table.

The box had come from yet another demon estate. The item in question looked like a pink, hollow ball.

"What is that thing?" Christine asked. "It looks like a hamster ball."

"It is," Nik said. "Sort of. Sometimes a demon child will keep pet rats or something similar."

"Huh," Christine said. "Is that why it has so much magical residue?"

"Yeah," Nik said. He wasn't about to explain that the estate had been from a particularly nasty demon who had a habit of shrinking down his enemies. The ball may have been used by his children for rats. Or it may have been used for tiny versions of enchanted demons.

There was a reason why Nik had been the only bidder on the estate's goods, as no one had really wanted to go through the mementoes from this particular demon.

"What can I help you with?" Nik asked after a moment. "I doubt you're here just to spend an afternoon doing inventory."

"You're right," Christine said with a sad, wistful smile. "Though being able to take an afternoon off does sound heavenly." She sighed. "No, I wanted to ask you about that magical book holder. It had held a collection of demon books, accounts of their battles. Do you still have it? Could I buy it from you?"

Nik immediately lied. "Nope. It sold fast," he said.

He was going to have to put it up for auction now, and then change the date of sale to be in the past.

"Okay," Christine said, seeming deflated. "I just thought…I'm looking for anything to help. You know?"

Nik nodded. "But I have to stay neutral," he told her gently.

"I know. That was why I offered to buy it, so that you would feel better about being neutral," Christine said. She gave him a crooked grin. "Unless there's something else that you think you should sell me instead?"

Nik wasn't sure of the expression on his face. His eyes and mouth were merely painted onto his wooden face. Magic gave him the ability to emote and express himself.

Given the puzzled look that Christine gave him, he was really going to have to redo those spells.

"I can't," Nik said. "I have to be more careful around

you, so that there isn't any hint of impropriety. I'm sorry. That's just the way it has to be."

Christine nodded. "Okay. I understand," she said, though she clearly didn't. "Thanks anyway."

Nik didn't have a soul that could ache. However, Christine had become a good friend over the years. And she looked so dejected.

It wouldn't ruffle his neutrality to make a suggestion to a friend, would it? Particularly a suggestion that came with strong warnings?

"Have you asked the oracles?" Nik asked.

Christine stopped and turned her head over her shoulder to look at him. "The oracles?"

Nik shrugged. "I don't know about troll oracles, if there are any. But you might go ask the human oracles what can be done to stop the war. Since it does concern humanity."

"Huh," Christine said. "I'd never thought about that. Where would I find them?"

Nik couldn't help but grin. "They've moved, actually. They used to be outside the city, at one of the hot springs. But when the place became overrun with tourists, locals would no longer go there for prophesy. So they moved to Ballard, to Bergen Place."

"Where?" Christine asked, obviously never having heard of this before, though she'd been born and raised in Seattle.

Then again, the changeling spell had kept her at home, afraid to go out and leave the house.

"It's at the intersection of Market Street and Leary, up in Ballard. You'll know it when you see it.

Collection of artistic trees on top of tall wooden poles."

"Thanks," Christine said. She straightened up, putting a determined look on her face. "I just need something. Anything. To help me stop this war."

"Good luck," Nik said. "One more thing. You'll need to be sure to take a human with you. The oracles won't address a troll alone."

Christine rolled her eyes. "Of course they won't," she said. "I'll bring Dennis or someone."

He didn't envy any oracle who denied Christine their wisdom. If she could win the war through sheer fierce determination, it would have already been won.

"And you need to be careful, too," Nik added. "They aren't dangerous," he assured her when she looked as if she'd start to growl at him. He would never have said anything about them to her if they were that bad. Particularly since she'd suggested taking her brother. "The oracles can play tricks with your mind. Your memory."

Before Christine could ask more, a subtle chine rang through the back room, letting Nik know that the next customer had arrived.

Nik opened up the backdoor to the emporium, located just past the shelves on the right-hand wall. He was the only one who could open or close that location. Christine gave him a sad smile and then walked out of the shop, back to the International District.

He put his own brave smile on when the smell of sulfur came rolling through the air. Though the demons had their own magic shops, they had seemed to have decided to all come to his.

Maybe they were hoping to run into Christine at some point.

They didn't realize just how fast starting anything in his shop would land them in deep trouble. Probably dead.

Nik and his emporium were *neutral*. No fighting was allowed in his shop. Period.

Or at least, Nik was trying to stay neutral. He had to. If he didn't, it would cost him his eternal life.

CHAPTER FIVE

King Garethen sighed as Phikathera, the royal treasurer, went on and *on* about how the king needed to release more funds. He shifted on his chair behind his great desk, carved out of a large boulder of granite. Though it was the perfect height for him in his chair, he still felt uncomfortable that afternoon.

The king met with the treasurer in his private study, a much more suitable location to talk about gold than the throne room. The room itself was tastefully done, with thin slits for windows on one wall overlooking the back gardens and a huge, beautiful purple geode hanging on the wall behind the king. The other walls held cases for scrolls and unusual stones.

Instead of sitting in one of the iron and leather chairs in front of the desk, Phikathera paced impatiently. The king was growing tired just watching her.

"Those are *our* trolls out there, fighting the demons, under the command of your heir," Phikathera pointed out. "They need the best equipment."

She was a pretty troll, with clear olive skin, a fire in her dark brown eyes, and gleaming white tusks. She followed the latest trend of the court and had gold rings piercing the upper parts of her tall pointed ears: three on the right side and two on the left. She wore a colorful black-and-red striped sleeveless tunic over a white blouse, and cropped black pants. Though the outfit itself was modest, it was made from the finest material money could buy, showing her wealth while not being ostentatious about it.

"I know our troops need good swords and axes," the king said, "but do we have to empty the vault to supply them? What about the axes and swords that they were originally equipped with? What has happened to them?"

"They were damaged during battle," Phikathera replied. "But—"

"Can they be repaired?" King Garthen asked, stubbornly sticking to the point.

"Some," Phikathera said slowly. She stopped her pacing and faced the king.

"Then shouldn't we focus on repairing broken equipment first rather than sending out all new?" the king asked. That sounded very reasonable to him.

Phikathera looked puzzled. "You do understand that most trolls, including your own guard, are very superstitious. If a weapon has already failed its owner once, what is to stop it from failing a second time? They need new swords and axes to give them confidence."

The king waved Phikathera's objection away. "Just tell them that the new equipment has been enhanced."

"Enhanced how?" Phikathera said, sounding stubborn.

"Get one of the priests down there and have them

bless every last weapon," the king said, pleased with his own cleverness.

Phikathera nodded slowly. "That might work. Though I don't think we should lie to our own trolls."

"We aren't lying," King Garthen said. "We're just saving the kingdom some expenses. What good is it to defend our home if there's nothing left when the war is over?"

"I don't like it," Phikathera said.

"You don't have to like it," the king said. "It's my decision. Your job is just to carry out my word and my will."

Phikathera cocked her head to one side, and her eyes took on a dreamy look, as though listening to a distant song, a melody half heard but never forgotten. "I will do as my king commands," Phikathera said after a few moments of utter stillness.

Then she stood back up straight and pointed to the small notebook on the king's desk. While a troll's memory was much better than a human's, the king had made a habit of noting down important things, just to jog his memory when he needed to. "However, I want you to remember my objections. And my warning that this is going to come back and bite us, later."

"Oh, I'll remember," the king said, reassuring Phikathera.

He always remembered insubordination.

Phikathera narrowed her eyes at him, as if seeking his true intent.

"Good," she said after a moment. "Then I will divide

the equipment budget, redirecting a third of the funds toward rehabilitation of older items."

"One half," King Garthen countered.

Again, that long pause, as if Phikathera was weighing the king's words.

"Fine, one half. Though I think you're being foolish," Phikathera warned. She turned abruptly and marched out the door without being dismissed.

King Garthen reached for his notebook, but then stopped, his hand frozen midway.

He didn't want to document such insubordination. He would remember.

The king sighed again and pushed his chair back from his desk, swinging his legs around and placing his feet on the cool granite desktop.

Then, and only then, did King Garthen allow himself to grin.

Phikathera didn't know about the *other* chests of gold that the king had stashed away. The ones that had come from that bargain with the cambion demons, granting them access to the fairy bridge, the one that connected Trollville to the human world. It could also be used to access other worlds, with the right incantations.

It wasn't that King Garthen was greedy. He'd never been greedy. Look at just how much he was spending on the army that they really didn't need! How much he spent on taking care of his citizens, maintaining the roads and such.

He was *saving* that other gold. Not keeping it for himself.

The humans had a funny saying about saving for a

rainy day. It had never made sense to the king. Rain was good. Rain watered the earth. Rain brought crops to fruition. Why would you save for a rainy day?

No, the king was saving those chests of gold for the day when the rains *didn't* come. Better to save in case of drought.

That way, he could spend more, even most, of the existing gold in the treasury. And still be prepared if something bad happened.

Much better to just keep the other gold hidden, or else Phikathera and the others would think of a way to spend it. Much better to save it for a rain-less day.

———

CHAPTER SIX

Beelzebub (known as Buddy to his friends) tried to ignore the words coming out of Samantha's mouth so he could get her back to doing *other* things with it. Much more important, at least as far as Buddy was concerned.

But the succubus, Sam, kept going on and on and fucking *on* about the war, how well their troops were doing, how the demons were soon going to be back on top of all the races where they belonged, how good it felt to actually be fighting (and winning).

As well as words of praise for Lars. How smart he was. How well his plans had worked. How handsome he was, though Sam had only seen him from a distance.

That was what finally put Buddy's back up and sent the front part of him, well, drooping.

"I was the one who gave Lars his troops, you know," Buddy reminded Sam when he could finally get a word in edgewise.

"You did?" Sam asked. Her wide black eyes blinked up

at him. She seemed surprised. "I remember Lars putting out a call, and how the little recruitment office was overrun with volunteers."

Buddy sighed and lay back on his bed, staring up at the smooth, black-glass ceiling. It took a simple spell to change the properties of it to be completely reflective so Buddy could watch himself in action. He still recalled that one time when he'd had the mirror images take physical shape so he'd had an orgy with himself.

Good times.

Right now, the ceiling reflected a vague image of Buddy, with his large nose, flabby lips, and ears that stuck on almost like wings on either side of his head. The moles and warts that covered his body were mere blemishes, and he couldn't see the hair sprouting out of them. His pot belly almost looked flat, something that amused him greatly, though his legs still appeared scrawny.

The bed itself was round so it was easy to place his partners exactly where he wanted them. Thick, soft rugs covered the floor (in case he didn't make it to the bed) and he'd padded the walls as well. He tried to be thoughtful of his companions.

"Yes, Lars did make a recruitment call. *After* he'd already started the war with my troops," Buddy said. "He didn't start the war with those volunteers, you know."

"Oh," Sam said. She sat up on the bed, her black eyes blinking as she considered. "Yes, that makes sense." She smiled at him, her blood-red lips outlining her white, pointed teeth. Her black, bat-like wings folded more tightly across her back as she settled down. She stuck her chest out at him, the nipples black against her pale skin.

"How smart of you to see the brilliance of Lars so early! Before he'd started the Great War!"

"Exactly," Buddy said. "Lars wouldn't be where he is today without the support of demons like me."

"Do you…" Sam paused, bit her lips, and looked away, coyly. "Do you think I could meet him someday?"

"Of course," Buddy said. He gave her a grin even though he felt like pounding his head against the nearest unpadded wall.

"That would be wonderful!" Sam said. "What do you think he likes?" she asked, her voice taking on a dreamy quality.

At least she'd gone back to her original actions, and was slowly stroking Buddy again.

"Do you think he'd like it rough? Or no, he'd prefer a softer partner, one he could be master over," Sam said, starting to sound a little breathless. Like she was getting off on the thought of being with Lars, instead of focusing on being with Buddy.

"You know, men talk about these things," Buddy said. Technically, that wasn't a lie. Men didn't necessarily talk about sex with each other as much as brag about it. "We compare things." Not just dick sizes, though that was frequently what went on in those sorts of conversations.

"Oh? Oh!" Sam said. She gave him a lascivious smile. "So I should do my best so that you can put in a good word for me?"

"Yes, exactly…oh," Buddy said as that mouth of hers *finally* stopped talking and got back down to business.

Later that night after Sam had gone, Buddy found himself unable to sleep despite how well the succubus had performed. Generally, after a session like that Buddy was hard pressed not to immediately pass out.

However, his brain kept going over not just what Sam had said, but the other things he'd heard. Like how many demons had raced to join Lars and the fighting once they'd started winning. And not just a few battles here and there, but major encounters. The reports that Lars sent to Buddy were torturous to read (kind of the point of any report). The text was small and dense, and Lars tended to bury the actual news on page three or even once, page seven.

The demons were winning the Great War.

Obviously, Buddy was going to have to have a talk with his own PR department to make sure that his name was more strongly linked with Lars'. Because in the grand scheme of things, it always made sense to be on the side of the winners, not the losers.

Though Buddy still had some queasiness over Lars and his wins. Unless that had been the *chile con queso* that he'd had for dinner.

Buddy gave a great belch, the sound echoing off the still-black ceiling. He patted his pot belly. It rumbled a moment under his scratchy palm, then settled back down.

Nope. Not the cheese. Must be Lars.

Buddy scratched himself idly as he pondered. It wasn't that he was upset that Lars was winning the war. Far from it. Like Sam, Buddy was looking forward to the day when the demons were finally back in charge of all the races, running things as they should be run. Buddy had plenty of ideas in that department, from the proper enslavement of humanity to how to punish those of the *kith and kin* who didn't immediately ally themselves with the demons.

But that was just it. Buddy had some ideas about how to do all of these things.

Lars had *plans*.

And not only that, Lars had plans that worked. With demons who, Buddy had to admit, were the least likely of any race to actually follow a plan. Worse than cats. And Buddy was quite fond of cats. No, demons were like the hellish variety of cats, who would come up and demand to be petted before turning and clawing the hand that was petting them.

What other plans did Lars have? Buddy had never given that much thought to after the war. He'd assumed that instead of winning, he'd be collecting Lars' soul. That had been the bargain, after all, in exchange for the troops.

Lars would demand a throne in Hell, to become one of the princes. The other demons would back him up.

Did Lars intend to take over Hell?

Of course he did. He was a demon.

However, Lars was a demon who planned.

He might succeed.

And what would happen to Buddy then? Would he be remembered as the demon who first helped Lars? The one who saw the general's brilliance early, before anyone else?

Or would he merely be a footnote, with some wag of a historian noting how his true importance was just as the creator of rock and roll? Or the influence of that famous song about the devil and sympathy?

That wouldn't do.

Buddy was a prince of hell. He might not look like one; he rarely acted like one. But he was damned if he was about to give up his throne to Lars.

Now, even Buddy wouldn't do something to affect the outcome of the war. He wanted to win as much as everyone else.

No, what he needed to do was to make sure that Lars understood the consequences of his actions. Whether he won or lost.

Time for the golden boy to pay a visit to Hell.

CHAPTER SEVEN

Vern hadn't expected that the magical council would meet in one of the government buildings in downtown Seattle. He'd expected some place more, well, magical. Not a room with a podium up front from where a representative could drone on like any politician, chairs and tables on either side where the council members sat, as well as such a large audience.

All in all, the room was very orange. The carpet was a red-orange, the walls a pumpkin orange, and the chairs a yellow orange. At least the long vertical shades pulled tightly across the windows on either side of the door were beige.

It felt very academic in some ways, like a room where a student might give a speech. Or three. All very normal and mundane. The air still had a touch of industrial cleaner, and was filled with muted conversation.

Although, Vern had to admit at least the audience was pretty swell. It was mostly composed of humans, though some of the *kith and kin* were there. Or at least, that was what

Vern thought that tall tree-like looking being in the corner was. And he thought he recognized some pixies as well: three-foot tall human-looking creatures with long skinny fingers, big eyes, and a big mouth full of sharp, pointed teeth.

However, most of the humans were *hippy* humans. The ones who didn't just mouth the phrase "keep Fremont weird" but who lived it. No bankers or software engineers here. Nope. Patchouli-wearing bearded men with long gauzy skirts—at least half a dozen of them—formed their own cluster in the middle of the front row. Many of the women wore leather bustiers that they kept threatening to spill out of, complete with leather pants and boots.

Why were some of them carrying wooden stakes and wearing crosses? Vern wasn't sure he wanted to know.

There were a few other old farts like him, more casually dressed, though the primary uniform tended to be T-shirts, jeans, loafers and no socks.

Vern felt decidedly out of place, though not uncomfortable. There were very few times in Vern's life when he could recall feeling uncomfortable in a social setting.

He still wished he'd been able to pass more of that ability along to Christine, his daughter, whether she was a troll or not.

"Hi, there," Vern said to the young woman who sat down in the empty seat next to him. "I'm Vern," he added, trying to put her at ease.

She looked over at him with big, scared eyes. Her blonde hair fell softly over her forehead, and her cheeks were round and pink, making her seem very young. She wore what Vern would call a "Little Bo Peep" costume—a white, short-sleeved blouse with puffy sleeves, a black, tightly laced corset that appeared to just be part of her outfit and not meant to show off her chest, a long blue-and-white gingham skirt and pointed black shoes.

He wanted to joke with her and ask her about her sheep, but she looked too scared. Maybe later.

"Hi," she said shyly. "This—this is my first time here," she said all in a rush.

"Same here," Vern admitted. "Was hoping that a youngster like you could show me the ropes."

The girl shook her head. "Should I go sit someplace else?" she asked, looking around the room. "So that someone different could sit here?"

"No, no, you're fine," Vern assured her. "We'll just have to learn the ropes together. Deal?"

"Deal," she said. "Oh, I'm Barbie, by the way."

"Nice to meet you," Vern said, nodding his head her direction.

He didn't offer to shake her hand. He no longer did that, not unless he absolutely had to. Though he'd been raised to be more demonstrative, and he still held hands with his wife every chance he got, ever since his magic had blossomed, it bothered him to touch strangers.

Blossomed. Bloomed. He could never think of another word for it. It wasn't that it hadn't been there before. Now that he knew what he was looking for, when he went searching for it inside of himself, he realized that it had always been there. Prior to being taught magic, the ability had been like a single bud on a scraggly rose bush, waiting for the right sunlight to be cast on it, the right amount of rain and soft winds.

Now, it was a full field of brilliant flowers, a greater resource to draw on than Vern would have ever imagined possible.

"What brings you here tonight, young Barbie?" Vern asked, curious. The girl seemed to still be shrunken in on herself. Why had she come here, to a crowded room, alone?

"The war," she said, her voice hoarse. "Isn't that why we're all here?"

"Possibly," Vern had to admit.

He had more insight into the war than most, given that it was his daughter, Christine, fighting it. However, he didn't see her regularly anymore. He missed the weekly Sunday dinners that they used to have. He tried to tell her how proud he was of her every chance he got, but that didn't seem to be enough to raise a smile from her anymore.

Christine would never say so out loud, but Vern suspected that the *kith and kin* were losing.

He'd developed his magic. Learned he had some real skill.

It was time for him to do his part for the war effort.

How could he put his talents to their best use, though?

Dennis, his son, had continued to recruit the *kith and kin* for Christine, as well as to sometimes talk those who wanted to leave the battles and turn away from Christine's troops into staying. He'd cut back on the hours of his job so he could do his part.

Vern felt bursting with pride for both his son and his

daughter. It probably radiated out from all the seams of his being.

As for his other daughter, Tina…she was still struggling. He'd tried to help her, but she wouldn't see him, not after that first time. She'd actually accused him of stealing all her magical ability.

Him! Vern would never steal anything. Not even a sucker from a demon baby.

So there had to be something else that Vern could do.

Just what, he wasn't sure. So he came to meeting tonight to hear what the council had to say, to find out how the humans and the magic council were supporting the war being fought by the *kith and kin* on the behalf of the humans.

Because once that first line of defense failed, the demons were coming after the humans.

And by then, it would be too late.

THE MEETING STARTED WITH THE COUNCIL ALL introducing themselves. Some of them, Vern would swear, were bankers. No software developers though.

The mix of twelve council members was more varied than the Seattle city council, which probably wasn't saying that much. It was at least half women, though Vern wasn't certain about the pronoun that was appropriate for the one individual sitting on the end of the table at the right. They had a full, luxurious black beard, yet at the same time, beautifully filled out a blue velvet evening gown— tall, thin, and buxom.

At least two of the council members appeared to be of south Asian heritage, based on the saris the women wore. There was one brown face who gave a First Nations name, and two black men. The rest, of course, were white and well to do.

Vern glanced at Barbie out of the corner of his eye. She appeared rapt, hanging on every word of the initial reading of the minutes from the last meeting.

He just couldn't get a read on her. Something about her seemed off to him. Possibly her age. When he thought about it, she struck him as someone much older than she appeared, though her hands looked as young and fresh as her face.

Or maybe it was how scared and shy she'd first appeared. Now that the meeting had started, all that fear had melted away and she looked eager and confident.

Finally the old business was all taken care of and they moved onto the agenda for the evening.

First up, the war.

"The Hunulary, Val'tian, and Rosinium have all been taken," said Thaxton, one of the banker-type men. "And battles have broken out between the Leafanders and Boxilays."

Vern nodded. He'd heard about the fallen three, but not the others. Christine had taken those losses personally, feeling as though she'd not moved in enough troops quickly enough.

She had no reliable crystal ball that she could use for reading the future. The demons continued to strike out in random places, or at least without a pattern that Christine and her generals had been able to read.

Kanishka, one of the Indian women, spoke up. "Wait, did you just say that the Leafanders and Boxilays were fighting? The demons? Or each other?"

Thaxton shrugged. "We aren't certain. There are definitely demons involved; however, there also appear to be troops of the Leafanders on the plane of the Boxilays."

Loud murmurs filled the audience.

Vern had no idea what that sort of fighting meant, though he could tell it was bad.

"What does that mean?" he asked out loud, as no one else appeared willing to fill in the blanks for the rest of them.

"Ah, we have some newcomers, yes?" Kanishka asked.

"Exactly," Vern said.

The woman gave him a quick, hard stare. Vern would say that his spidey-sense tingled abruptly, as if she was testing him magically for a moment.

The feeling passed with a cascade of goosebumps down his spine.

Kanishka blinked, then nodded. "Welcome," she said. "What it means is that the *kith and kin* are turning against each other."

"Or it means that the Leafanders have allied themselves with the demons in order to prevent themselves from being annihilated," another council member pointed out.

"What's the difference?" Kanishka said. "We don't know, and will never know, the true cause of their feud. Just the outcome."

Vern bobbed his head to side to side. He did but didn't agree with Kanishka. While the outcome did matter more, why that particular group of the *kith and kin* had started fighting might be relevant to how to get them to stop.

Reluctant allies could possibly be turned again. Though never trusted. Not fully.

"We continue to send magical supplies up the line," Thaxton continued, reading from his notes. "The latest batch of protection charms and magically enhanced armor were well received and much appreciated."

Vern felt himself perk up. The humans were supplying artifacts? Cool. Maybe that was a way he could help the war effort, to go and enchant something for the troops.

He was aware that enchanting anything took a lot of effort, between the ingredients as well as the magical power. But he was up to the task.

"Reports of demons on the human plane continue to skyrocket," Thaxton continued. "They haven't amassed in any single location that we can track. But they keep coming. Many of them appear to be traveling over the fairy bridge, located in the Arboretum."

Vern frowned at that. Christine was responsible for that bridge. She'd strengthened the defenses of it specifically so that it would turn away any demons trying to cross it.

Were the reports wrong? Or was there something wrong with the bridge? He was going to have to check.

And why hadn't anyone told Christine about this?

Thaxton then listed the battles that had been won, the *kith and kin* races that had been saved, or at least, the demon attacks fended off.

Many more battles were reported as won than as lost.

Given the way that Thaxton was phrasing things, it appeared more hopeful than Christine had been saying.

Was the war actually going well?

While Thaxton read out a list of needed supplies, Vern thought about it. No, the war was still going badly. The battles that had been won were merely singular skirmishes. On the losing side of the equation, they'd lost entire races and planes of existence to the demons. Fewer lost battles were being reported, but the ones that they had lost were massive compared to the many tiny fights that had been won.

When Thaxton finished his report, Kanishka spoke up. "Since we have some newcomers in the audience, I will open a five-minute discussion time and take questions from the audience."

Barbie's hand shot up, like an A-student who desperately wanted to answer the teacher's questions.

Kanishka nodded to her.

"Why are we doing this?" Barbie asked.

She sounded innocent enough, but Vern felt something uneasy stirring in his gut. Surely this question had been asked and answered before, many times over.

"Can you be more specific?" Kanishka said.

"Why are we sending all these supplies to the *kith and kin*?" Barbie said. "With all the reports of demon activity in our city, and there's been a lot of that, why aren't we more focused on protecting our own?"

"We *are* protecting our own, as you so quaintly put it," said the being with the black beard and the blue dress—Kim as they had introduced themselves as. "By supporting the *kith and kin*, we are keeping the demons from overrunning the human plane."

"The traditional allies of the *kith and kin* are the demons, not the humans," Barbie pointed out.

"Not all of the *kith and kin* races accept that," Thaxton replied.

"True. However, we need to start focusing more on the *human* race," Barbie said. "The only way to protect our world is to start closing the portals. How long have we allowed the divert treaty to be perverted? We need to petition the Host, right now, to change the treaty and close our borders to anyone who isn't human."

The bearded men in the long skirts all seemed outraged at such a suggestion. As did some of the leather-clad women.

But Vern felt that far too many agreed with Barbie. It was the nature of the world just then—I have mine and I'm not about to share.

"For those of you newcomers," Kanishka said, raising her voice to drown out those who had started chattering, "DHIVRT stands for the Demon-Human Interaction and Visitation Rights treaty."

"The demons are breaking the treaty by coming here, particularly in the large numbers that have been reported," Barbie pointed out. "This is a matter for the Host. Not the council. The council should be more concerned with protecting the humans in its jurisdiction. Not suppling the *kith and kin*, who will turn on us and ally themselves with the demons when push comes to shove."

Kanishka tried to cut off the loud uproar. "The council

voted to ally themselves with the *kith and kin* in the war effort—"

"We need a new vote!" Barbie said, her voice booming across the room. "We need to block them! All of them! Stop the invaders! New vote! New vote!"

Several members of the audience picked up the chant.

"New vote! New vote! New vote!"

Vern just shook his head. There was no way that this was going to end well.

KANISHKA WAS FINALLY ABLE TO REGAIN CONTROL OF the meeting. "There is a procedure for petitioning the council to exercise a vote," she said sternly. "Disrupting a council meeting is not the proper way."

Barbie still sat beside Vern, looking unabashed. Her cheeks glowed from all the excitement. A holy fervor burned in her eyes.

Vern felt as though he'd been surprised by a deadly viper in sheep's clothing, or some such analogy.

"You need to craft a proposal, then get the proper number of signatures from the citizens in order to petition the council," Kanishka continued.

"Exactly," Barbie said, standing once again. From a magical pocket that she carved out beside her, Barbie pulled a large collection of papers. "Here is the paperwork, as well as all the signatures," she said, holding them up. "May I present them to the council?"

Vern felt rather than heard the sigh from Kanishka. She'd been sandbagged. Again. He felt sorry for her.

"You may," Kanishka said. "At the end of the meeting," she added before Barbie could approach the group, "when I call for new business."

Barbie pouted and sat back down, her moment of glory diverted.

Vern smiled and nodded at Kanishka. He was really starting to like her.

The council members went through the rest of the agenda quickly, covering things like expanding the search among the homeless for those who were magically gifted, supplying tuition for the magical who needed extra training, and the start of the planning for the equinox celebration.

Kim gave the report on the studies of the corruption crystals. Mainly, no one had yet figured out how to counteract the effect on the humans. Since they weren't specifically outlawed by the DHIVRT treaty, there wasn't anyone the humans could appeal to.

Vern didn't like the predatory smile Barbie gave at that news.

Just another piece of information that she'd use in her efforts to "purify" the human plane, he knew.

Finally, when everything on the agenda had been covered, Kanishka called for any new business. Barbie raised her hand again, not like an A-student eager to please, but like the smart-ass in the class who had all the answers.

"You may approach the council," Kanishka said, "and present your petition."

Barbie gave a smug smile to the entire room as she

slipped out of the row of seats and handed her papers to the secretary for the council.

"We will need to verify the signatures," Kanishka said after the secretary had glanced through the sheaf in front of him and then nodded. "After they've been validated, we will schedule a new vote. If there's nothing else, this meeting is now dismissed."

Vern felt himself recoiling from the anger now radiating from Barbie. He didn't like the dark look that she shot Kanishka. She'd really wanted her time in the spotlight again, and Kanishka had just denied it.

As quickly as possible, Vern got out of the meeting room.

He'd found what he'd come for.

And though he had never expected it, it appeared that the best place to put his talents seemed to be into politics, to make sure that the council didn't vote to cut back the lines of supplies to the *kith and kin*.

After he went to check out what was happening on the fairy bridge.

CHAPTER EIGHT

Ty Brooks, demon hunter extraordinaire, finally felt ready to join the fray again. He'd been severely poisoned while fighting a demon. His black skin no longer had that ashy hue, his arms had stopped shaking after he finished a sparring session with his great sword, and his keen sense of smell had finally returned to him when he shifted from his human form to that of a partial wolf. (He was only one-quarter wolf and had spent some serious time training as a youth, so he wasn't tied to the cycle of the moon like his werewolf mother and could change at will.)

He'd taken himself to the bailiff's office, intending to see what was on the charts, possibly plan out his next gig.

What he saw on the wanted board in the hallway sent his hackles rising and a low growl rumbling in his chest.

He pulled the poster for Lars Sorgenfreys off the wanted board and stomped down the hallway to the bailiff's office, making a beeline toward the clerk in charge of keeping the wanted posters up to date.

"What the hell is this?" Ty demanded, slapping the wanted poster down on the clerk's desk.

"It's a poster declaring that Lars Sorgenfreys is a wanted demon," the clerk said slowly, as if trying to explain something to an overactive two year old.

The clerk looked like a cross between a ram and a human, with a ram-like face and great tusks curled up around his ears, a tall thin body, and knees that operated backwards.

"I know that it's a poster for Lars. Why did someone strike through it, lowering the priority for his capture?" Ty asked. "He's the head of the demons leading the attack against the *kith and kin*!"

The ram-headed clerk—Gerald, according to the nameplate on his desk—heaved a great sigh. He sat back in his chair and chewed his cud for a moment before he finally looked back up at Ty.

"His activities in the Great War have nothing to do with his wanted status," Gerald explained. "Unless you have documented proof that since his escape he's personally attacked, maimed, or otherwise harmed another being."

Ty blinked, feeling the world under his feet shifting. "So leading armies, directing them to attack and decimating entire races of the *kith and kin* is not enough to keep his rating higher?"

"The law doesn't cover that," Gerald said with a shrug. "It was never meant to cover such an extreme. It was put into place to stop escaped demons who were rampaging through the human population. Not the ones who hid and remained in hiding, technically never hurting a fly."

Ty was at a complete loss of words. "So you lowered the priority for his capture?" was all he could manage.

The clerk shrugged again. "That's the law. After ninety days, if a demon hasn't done any direct, provable harm, their priority gets marked down. The poster won't be removed from the board, though. So you can still hunt him."

"But the court will stop assigning people to go after him," Ty pointed out. And while yes, that meant that there was less competition for him, it still meant that Lars was more likely to stay free for a longer period of time.

"True," Gerald said. "But there isn't anything I can do. My hands are tied."

Ty wanted to insist that the clerk print out a new poster, one with the original priority. He wanted to go petition the court to start a new demon-hunt, one that was focused on finding Lars and putting him back into prison.

He wanted a lot of things that were never going to happen, like for his own people, the lycanthropes and those who generally called themselves werewolves, to stop bickering amongst themselves and go join the *kith and kin* who were fighting the war.

None of that was going to happen, though.

Instead, he turned and marched out of the bailiff's office. He wasn't going to share this news with Christine. She had enough on her plate already.

Nope. It was time for him to get back into action. Sure, the trail was colder than hell when it came to finding Lars.

Ty was just going to have to go seeking the demon

other ways. Paying visits to some shady characters. Maybe even laying out a bribe or two.

While many in Ty's clan considered him an abomination, as he'd been born from a lycanthropic mother and a human father, he still knew a few who would talk with him.

They would have news.

Now, he just had to get his hands on some fresh goat meat.

CHAPTER NINE

Dennis strode down Madison Street in Capitol Hill, heading toward his next meeting. He'd changed out of his work clothes—nice shirt, chinos, loafers—and into what he'd come to call his game clothes—Seahawks jersey, jeans, and beat up boots.

It wasn't that Dennis had never been a 'hawks fan. He'd always followed the games, but he'd never been a great believer in the religion, had never owned a jersey or any other accoutrement. He still wasn't that much of a follower, actually. However, since he'd turned into Christine's primary recruiter, he'd discovered that most of the *kith and kin* were into sports. Not necessarily human sports, but their own twisted and wonderful varieties of it.

Wearing a Seahawks jersey made the *kith and kin* who he was meeting feel more at ease, as if they already had something in common.

Tonight, Dennis was meeting with Christine first before he went out on his usual rounds. There were several restaurants and bars on Capitol Hill who catered expressly to the *kith and kin*. Dennis had gotten to know many of them, and was considered a regular at half a dozen or so.

When Dennis had realized that he was starting to put on weight from all the alcohol he'd been consuming, he'd switched to plain soda water. Many of the bartenders would put in a shot of something colored for him, so that it appeared he was still drinking liquor even when he wasn't, just one more thing Dennis had gotten good at—appearing to be loosely drunk while he still had all of his wits around him.

A posse of street kids lined the edge of the sidewalk outside the restaurant. Dennis had no magical abilities whatsoever (and that still pissed him off sometimes), so he edged around the group carefully.

Were there members of the *kith and kin* mixed in with the humans? Or something else?

Dennis paused at the door to the restaurant while a group of drunk secretaries came out. He glanced over his shoulder and waited for the entire gaggle to come tumbling out.

One of the young men stared hungrily at Dennis. He had blond hair that was probably past the point of washing and should just be shaved off, full cheeks as if he'd never missed a meal, with a contrasting sharp nose and thin lips. He wore the usual street kid clothes, dirty T-shirt, vest, stained jeans with huge tears across the knees, brown sneakers without any laces in them.

While Dennis looked, the kid barred his teeth. Dennis wasn't close enough to hear the growl, but he still knew it was being sounded. Damned kid was either part demon or possessed.

Dennis felt his back stiffen. His immediate urge was to go and confront the kid, demand to know who he was looking at. Probably get into some sort of scuffle.

Dennis had, after all, been *born* ready.

However, getting into that sort of fight was the surest way for him to lose the respect of Christine, as well as the beings he was working so desperately hard to recruit.

Funny how his sister's opinion of him was actually more important.

"See ya," Dennis said with a casual wave of his hand before he turned and went into the restaurant.

He'd also learned the best way to truly piss off a demon was to treat them like they were inconsequential. To not engage as if they *mattered*, but to brush them off like lint.

On the scorecard Dennis kept in his head, he knew that he'd just notched another tiny win.

He would admit that he still had bad nights, nights when he felt as though he was completely inconsequential, that he'd never mattered to anyone, not his parents, his sister, even his friends (particularly the ones who stopped calling or trying to get together when he got busy. The ones who he still regularly texted and chatted with—he now knew they were gold. They were a smaller group than he'd like to consider, but they still had his back.)

Just as he had his sister's back.

Christine was in her full-on human guise. She still looked kinda like the girl he'd grown up with. At least that horrible mop of curly brown hair was gone—really, she never should have listened to Tina and gotten that perm. Her skin was darker colored than his or anyone else in the family. She had the same high, round cheeks that he did, the same small nose and wide-set eyes.

She held herself differently now. Her posture was better and she no longer looked as though she wanted to hide constantly. She looked out across the room, assessing threats and allies with equal skill.

She'd really grown up nice. He was proud of her.

Now, if only they could find a good troll boyfriend for her…

After the war.

She also wore clothes that suited her more than she used to. He couldn't recall any specific outfits that she'd worn before, just the general impression that she'd always had on baggy things and had been trying to hide herself.

Tonight, she wore a tight, white sleeveless shirt that was something between a camisole and a muscle shirt. He wouldn't be surprised if she was also wearing a short skirt, something that showed off her legs, whereas before she would have been all covered up.

While she wasn't his type—he preferred runners to wrestlers—he could understand the appeal.

Dennis wove his way through the scattered booths and tables, seating himself next to Christine. The restaurant seemed really loud to him—he was surprised that Christine had suggested it. Even if they did serve some of the best Mexican food in Seattle.

Before he could say anything, a waitress came up with a large goblet containing a blue margarita.

"What can I get you?" she asked, turning to smile at Dennis.

"One of those," Dennis said, indicating Christine's drink.

"Right away," the waitress said, hurrying away.

"You okay?" Dennis asked after Christine had taken a large swig of the drink in front of her. He helped himself to some of the chips and salsa already on the table.

Wow. The chips were made in house—fresh, crunchy, tangy and salty. Plus the salsa was amazing.

Christine sighed and nodded, then rolled her shoulders. "Yeah. It's just been one of those days, you know?"

"You're having a lot of those," Dennis said. The war hadn't been going well. In fact, now that he thought about it, Christine had been having large amounts of alcohol every time he'd seen her recently.

"Yeah," Christine said, taking another swig.

How did alcohol affect a troll? Dennis didn't recall ever seeing Christine drunk. He had to remember that though as a human she was about the same height as he was, as a troll, she was actually much taller and bigger.

"But I might have some good news," Christine said after a moment.

"Really?" Dennis said, surprised. "That's awesome!" Had someone else joined Christine's side? Had they just won a major battle?

"I hope you'll still think so in a bit," Christine said.

"Huh?" Dennis asked. He didn't like the serious look on Christine's face. "What's up?"

"I'm going to need your help. Tonight," Christine said.

"Sure! Whatcha need?" Dennis said easily. He started switching around appointments in his head. He could go see the rowdy boys tomorrow night, and possibly schedule a happy hour with the Sonicasm later in the week, and maybe…

"Excuse me?" Dennis asked when he realized that Christine had kept talking and had just mentioned something about oracles.

"I need you to come with me to visit the oracles tonight," Christine said.

Dennis blinked. "Why me?" he asked. Shit. Was there some strange cult thing she was going to be asking him to do? Maybe she needed him to be some sort of sacrificial lamb?

Christine blew out a frustrated breath. "Because. They're the damned *human* oracles. They won't address me. And there aren't any oracles in Trollville, or who specialize in just troll futures. The ones I found are more general, and just foretell things for the *kith and kin*."

"So what exactly do you need me to do?" Dennis asked.

"We need to go up into Ballard later," Christine said. "Probably around midnight. Then I'd like you to ask the oracles what we need, exactly, in order to win the war."

"Why hasn't anyone asked them before this?" Dennis said, confused. It seemed like such an obvious thing to do. "I mean, if they have the information, why don't they just tell us?"

Christine gave a snort. "I think it's in their damned handbook to never give a straight answer to any question," she said. "They're always obscure and they use a lot of weasel words so that even if whatever they've predicted never occurs, they can still claim that they're right."

"Sound like con men to me," Dennis said.

"Exactly," Christine said. "And that's why I think you'll be the best man for the job."

"Thanks, I think," Dennis said sharply. What, did Christine really think of him as someone who lied for a living?

Then again, he did sometimes stretch the truth. A little. In places.

"Why don't you ask Dad?" Dennis said after their waitress came back and deposited Dennis's drink in front of him.

Christine gave another expressive sigh. Really, it was fascinating how well he could read those, even given the current noise levels.

This one was less frustrated, more worried.

"Dad's...changed since he really started practicing magic, you know?" she said after a moment.

"I'll say," Dennis replied. Dad *had* changed. He was still goofy, but he seemed to get lost inside his head more. He'd explained it—he said that he just seemed to notice so much more of the world now that he got distracted by it more easily.

"Besides, Dad had a meeting tonight. Some sort of caucus," Christine added.

"And we have to go tonight because?" Dennis asked.

"Because the oracles only have a few open spots whenever they show up. Most of their time is already taken up by people on the list," Christine explained.

"Will they have time to talk to us?" Dennis said. "Or will we have to go on a waiting list for some future time?"

"They'll talk to us," Christine growled. "I'll make damned sure of it."

Dennis forced a smile onto his face. He'd never expected to be intimidated by his own sister before. Or hell, even scared by her. "There's my shy librarian," Dennis teased, forcing his own smile.

For a moment, Dennis worried that he'd gone too far. Christine's face took on a menacing glare. He could tell that she considered punching him.

"Sis?" Dennis said, uncertain.

Christine shook her head, all the anger flowing out of her. She gave him a half smile. "Thanks," she said softly. "I needed that, more than you realize."

"What's going on?" Dennis said. "No, really. What's going on? What's got you so tightly wound up?"

"You know we're losing the war, right?" Christine said. "I'm running out of options here. And warriors. And ideas. I need some help. Quickly. And right now, every death, every loss, is just getting more and more personal."

Dennis nodded, worried. He'd known on an intellectual level that the war was going to change his sister. He should have realized that, at least while it was still going on, she would grow darker.

"It's okay," Dennis said.

Christine glared at him.

"No, really," Dennis said. "It would completely totally suck for most of humanity if you did lose. I get that. And I'm sure that you're going to blame yourself no matter what happens. However, I know you. You will do your best, and beyond. No one could ask any more."

Christine blinked.

Wait, were those tears in her eyes?

She sniffed. "You're demented."

"Look who's calling who crazy," he replied immediately.

Christine snorted. "Yeah, there is that." She gave him a smile, a true smile, probably the first one she'd given him all evening. "Thanks," she said again.

"You're welcome," Dennis said.

The waitress came back and they ordered hot, spicy Mexican food. When Christine left to use the restroom, Dennis took a deep breath, realizing that he'd just taken on yet another task for the war beyond recruiting individuals for Christine.

It wasn't to remind Christine of what she was fighting for. She saw that every time she came back to the human plane.

No, it was to keep Christine from doubting herself. She was already giving her all.

He just had to make sure that she didn't lose herself in the process.

CHAPTER TEN

Though it was only a Tuesday night, there were still large crowds of people on Market Street in Ballard, moving from one restaurant or bar to the next. Then again, August had been beastly hot, and it was only cool at night. While some of the swarming crowd were probably locals, most of them appeared to be tourists, at least to Christine's practiced eye.

She was pretty sure that it was an all human crowd. Since the war had started, the *kith and kin* had stopped coming across the bridge to just visit. Most beings were either actively fighting or building up their barricades and reserves.

Normally, it was difficult for demons or for anyone who wasn't a member of a *kith and kin* race to get to a closed plane that was defined as a home world. However, that damned corrupted eruption spell that the demons had come up with had been very effective in transporting armies to places where they shouldn't have been able to go.

No place was safe. That pissed Christine off more than most anything else.

However, it wasn't just the eruption spell. The demons were tunneling through to other planes, too. No one had been able to figure out just how they were doing it.

Fortunately, none of the demons had felt like challenging her that evening. Or rather, fortunate for them. Christine was in no mood for any of their shit. She'd seen the one hanging out with the posse of street kids outside the Mexican restaurant on Capitol Hill. Others had popped up throughout the night. She assumed they were part of an informal spy network that tracked her every movement.

If only she could find Lars. She had no idea if she'd be able to beat him in combat. He was likely to cheat and wouldn't attack her by himself.

That was okay. She might have come up with a few plans and scenarios herself for when they finally did meet.

She knew that Ty was still hunting for Lars. She'd informed the demon hunter to not engage Lars when he did find the demon, but to just signal her.

Christine did have people watching the Sorgenfreys' house, but no one had seen Lars go in or out of it. Then again, there were probably portals inside the house that allowed Lars as well as anyone meeting him free access.

No one would believe Christine when she told them that Lars was hiding in plain sight on the human plane. But she knew that was where he was.

Too bad she couldn't just storm the place. It wouldn't have been that difficult to arrange. However, it would have been useless, as once they started the process, Lars would have slipped away through a portal.

Dennis walked beside Christine. He looked a little out of place in his Seahawks jersey, particularly in a place as hippy as this. She understood why Dennis had changed into it before meeting her at the restaurant. She appreciated his efforts more than she could say. He was a big reason why her side was still afloat in terms of the battles.

Without him, they might have been wiped out already.

Christine was glad that she'd chosen to wear a white sleeveless tank top that night, along with a pair of black shorts with a cute twirly skirt over them. They might not be the most trendy thing on the market, but if she needed to fight, she'd rather not be hemmed in by modesty. Particularly on the human plane.

They'd had to park several blocks away from their destination. Christine was sweating just from the short walk. She was going to be so glad when this summer was over. At least they'd been able to walk past the Ballard library. Such a nice building, with a green garden on top.

There were days when Christine missed being an archivist librarian. Having set hours, set tasks. Limited people contact.

As they walked, Dennis had kept up a running commentary about the various *kith and kin* races that he'd been meeting with. She gave him some tips about communicating with the others.

Finally, they turned the corner, going down Twenty-

Second Avenue towards Market Street, and Christine could see the line of tree statues.

The park was an odd triangle-shaped piece of land where five streets came together. Christine had read that it had been dedicated to the city of Bergen in Norway, and that more than one king of Norway had flown over to recognize the place.

She'd wondered, more than once, about getting someplace on the human plane dedicated to Trollville. Besides the troll under the Fremont bridge.

Maybe she'd have to try and sanctify it someday. Or something. She wasn't quite sure how that worked.

All of the wooden poles holding up the trees themselves had a faint blue, magical tinge to them. There were surely portals set up between at least four of them. But which one went to the oracles?

Sitting on top of the five poles were various artistic representations of trees. The first one looked like a child's rendition of a tree, with a plain wooden trunk and five individual tall leaves sticking up out of the branches like a weird hand.

Beside it was a tree made up of great blue-and-white porcelain balloons, looking more like a group of jellyfish tied to a wooden pole rather than a tree.

Christine sighed. She'd never be able to understand abstract art, let alone *human* art. She'd always taken that as a personal failing until she finally figured out that she wasn't actually human.

At least the statue next to the jellyfish looked almost like a tree—more like a round pine tree made out of clam shells. And the one after that also looked pretty tree like.

The last one though was just a thumb of concrete sticking up on top of the pole.

"They're all different representations of trees," Dennis said, reading from his phone. "An immigrant tree, a primordial tree, stuff like that."

"Okay," Christine said. She'd have to go do research later.

She remembered a time when she loved doing research, looked forward to it on a regular basis. That old life seemed so far away from her now…

A placard standing on the corner caught her eye. It advertised a walking tour of Ballard.

"Want to go on a tour?" Dennis snerked as he came up beside her.

Christine silently pointed to the bottom right corner of the sign. The tour was led by the Oracles of Seattle, LLC. Their logo was a pyramid with an eye floating just above the point.

"So, you folks here to take the tour?" came a voice from behind them.

Christine glanced over her shoulder, then straightened up and turned right around. She barely contained her growl. Her claws wanted to shoot right out. Where was her ax?

The being wasn't an angel, but was probably related. She shone with her own light, disturbingly bright. She had on a neon-fuchsia T-shirt that proclaimed "Tour Guide" across her ample chest. Her blonde-brown hair was tied up in a ponytail, her skin sun-kissed. She looked to be in her late twenties, though Christine suspected that her actual age was probably more like two hundred years old.

The *kith and kin*'s usual allies were the demons, so they were most comfortable with those types of beings. Angels were very disturbing for all of the *kith and kin*. Christine had met a couple, and while she didn't have nightmares about them, she really never wanted to repeat the experience.

"Hi," Dennis said shyly. "Yes, we would like to take the tour."

The being gave Dennis a blinding smile that set Christine's own teeth on edge. "*You* would be most welcome," she said directly to Dennis in a voice that probably sounded like honey to him. "And you?" she said, turning to frown at Christine, her voice now holding a distinct edge.

Christine forced herself to smile instead of seeing whether or not her tusks could tear this creature's throat out before she had a chance to fight back.

"I am Princess Kizalynn Linumok Te'Dur," Christine said, announcing herself. "*We* have a question to put before the oracle."

Christine got an immense sense of satisfaction from the confusion that flowed across the being's face.

"She's my sister," Dennis proclaimed proudly.

"I see," the being said, still looking confused. "I need to verify that we have enough tickets and that we aren't sold out. Just a second."

She turned and hurried away.

"Wow," Dennis said, unable to take his eyes off her perfect bottom. "Where do I sign up for something like that?"

"She's part angel, dummy," Christine pointed out, still

unsettled. "She wouldn't have anything to do with you." She hadn't meant for the words to come out in such a growl, but she was still unsettled.

"Oh," Dennis said. "Too important for me, huh?"

"Huh?" Christine responded, completely confused. "No. It has nothing to do with your rank or your family. She isn't human. What's gotten into you?"

Dennis heaved a heavy sigh. "Nothing. I'm fine," Dennis said, pasting an obviously fake smile on his face. "Do you think they'll let us in?"

"They better," Christine growled.

"Ah, Princess Kizalynn," came a new masculine voice that was just as disturbing as the girl's had been.

Christine plastered a smile on her face and turned. The man looked older than the girl. Maybe mid-fifties, Asian, and just as fucking annoying, setting Christine's back right up just with his presence. He wore the same neon-pink T-shirt and carried a clipboard. His black hair was shaved on one side of his head, the hair on the other half flopping over. Speckles of gray glinted in the streetlights. He wore a bright silver whistle around his neck, like what a coach would use.

"Yes?" Christine said when the man didn't continue.

"It is such an honor to meet you," the man said earnestly. "My name's Ko San. This is Laurie. The great oracle Toby announced earlier that an unexpected visitor would arrive tonight, and that we should escort you directly to him."

"Really?" Christine asked, surprised. Normally, any proclamation by the oracles wasn't that clear.

Then again, if he'd just proclaimed an "important

visitor" was coming by, he could have then declared that anyone showing up was *important*.

She glanced over at Dennis, but he only had eyes for Laurie.

While Laurie appeared to be giving Dennis a shy smile in return.

Ah, shit.

Well, at least Christine only liked trolls and wasn't going to be bringing a demon home for dinner anytime soon.

THEY HAD TO WAIT FOR ANOTHER FIFTEEN MINUTES until it was time for the tour to start. Dennis and Christine wandered around the small park, reading the plaques on all the trees

The plaque for the jellyfish tree—also known as the immigration tree—described how Chinese porcelain and Danish patterns intermingled. It made sense to Christine, as most human families really did intermingle a lot. Troll families didn't, at least not according to her bio dad, Te'Dur.

He found it perfectly reasonable that she preferred trolls to any other being in terms of a mate. Trolls tended to be that way. There weren't many troll families who were mixed. Unlike, say, orcs, elves, giants, or even fairies. Brownies and pixies also tended to be homogeneous.

All the history and genetics had fascinated Christine, who'd wanted to learn more, but of course, there were no histories or ethnobiographies.

When this damned war was over, she was planning on funding an entire college to do that sort of study.

In the meanwhile, she had to put up with Dennis sighing every time he spotted Laurie standing next to the tour sign, trying to get more people to sign up.

"You know, you could ask for her number," Christine told him.

Dennis looked at her, surprised. "You said she wouldn't go out with me."

She shrugged. "How will you know if you don't try?"

"You think I have a chance?" Dennis asked, his eyes wide.

"What, are you suddenly twelve years old?" Christine said. "Why are you scared?"

"Because she's perfect," Dennis said breathlessly.

"You understand that I'm never going to be able to see that," Christine said in an effort to not roll her eyes too hard. "But she might be amenable, given the looks she's been giving you."

"She's been looking at me?" Dennis asked, still sounding breathless.

Christine glared at him when he gave her a big grin, obviously teasing her back.

"I will ask her out, after the tour," Dennis assured Christine. "After the tour." He sounded confident for once.

"No, now," Christine said. "You don't know if she'll still be here at the end of the tour."

"Really?" Dennis said, doubt shading his voice. "What if she says no?"

"Then you'll know," Christine told him. "And you

won't spend the rest of your life wondering, or regretting that you let the perfect one get away. Life's just too damned short."

Dennis speared her with a sharp look. Then he nodded. "You're right." He straightened his back, growing tall and strong, then he marched over to where Laurie was still standing, like a soldier going into battle.

From where Christine stood, it appeared as though the conversation was going fairly well. At least it appeared that Laurie hadn't shot Dennis down right away.

Still, he was still partially slumped over as he walked back over to her.

"She said it will depend on what the great oracle Toby says," Dennis told Christine.

Christine shook her head, puzzled. What the hell did that have to do with anything?

"It seems that she's related to the oracle, like a second cousin or something," Dennis continued.

"Huh," Christine said. Did that mean that the oracles were related to angels? Were they beings of light? She'd figured that these oracles were just special humans, maybe some type of human magician, since they only dealt with human fates.

"Well, it looks as though you won't have to wait for long," Christine said as Ko San blew on his whistle, the signal that the tour was about to start.

There were actually two tours being led that night. Ko San would lead the smaller group, with only about six people in it total, including Dennis and Christine, while Laurie led the other, larger group.

Was only Ko San's group going to talk with the

oracles? It made sense. The rest of them were human, and for the most part not magical, at least as far as Christine could see.

"We will start at this end," Ko San said, leading them to one end of the line of trees, the fossil tree. "These statues were commissioned from the artist Jenn Lee Dixon to commemorate…"

The words faded, though Christine was trying to pay attention. But someone else was calling her. Not by name. Just something that demanded the focus of her inner being. Christine closed her eyes for a moment so she could listen better.

A bell-like tone sounded, deep in her bones. It reminded her of the bell that rang when she made a promise, the oath being recorded deep within the earth.

You have been summoned.

Christine started, opening her eyes again. She glanced quickly at Dennis. He gave her a wide-eyed look, then nodded.

Seemed he'd heard something similar.

The space between the fossil tree and the tree standing next to it briefly lit up. It reminded Christine of that weird lens flare that was so popular with certain movie directors.

She shook her head. Bad special effects just added to her already poor opinion of the oracles.

Still, Dennis took a step forward in that direction. He must have seen it too. The rest of the people on the tour seemed oblivious, fascinated by Ko San droning on and on.

Christine recognized the magic suddenly. It was a

minor spell, but he drew all eyes to him, so that no onlooker would see them step away.

At least the beings running this tour appeared to have their shit together.

Christine checked again with Dennis. He nodded at her.

Together, they stepped between the two trees, and into someplace else.

———

CHRISTINE COUGHED AND BLINKED HER EYES. IT reminded her of that one time Tina had talked her into going to a sauna. The heat wrapped around her like a wet blanket, heavy and oppressive. Billows of steam rose up in front of her, blocking the view, making her an easy target. White subway tiles covered the wall she could see, hard and clinical. The air smelled of salt and lemon, like a cheap bar that served tequila by the jug.

Someone behind them cleared their throat.

Christine jumped around immediately, raising her hands. Only then did she realize that the illusion of her human body had been stripped away. She stood as herself, muscles, claws, tusks, and all.

Dennis stood beside her, fully human. He looked younger than he usually did, his face broad and open.

Was that his true self? So trusting? She'd always thought of him as more of a cynic.

Guess he really did have hope and optimism, as she once did. Before the war.

Behind them, a young man sat alone on a ledge

coming out from the wall, leaning back. He had black hair that fell over his gray-green eyes like a bad-boy wannabe, light brown skin that could speak either of African American heritage or just a really good tan, a round face that was both young and old at the same time. Maybe it was the light in his eyes that seemed to spear Christine's very soul.

He wore just a white towel wrapped around his waist as he lounged in the steam room. Tattoos covered his arms in complete sleeves, though his chest and neck were bare. Christine found her eyes darting toward the ink as she could swear she just saw one of the brilliant hibiscus flowers on his bicep open further.

"Ah, princess," the oracle Toby said. "Good to see you again."

"Have we met?" Christine asked. She belatedly lowered her clawed hands and straightened up, no longer in a fighting pose.

Toby gave her a huge grin and bobbed his head slightly. "In a way," he said. "I wasn't the one who set your Destiny, but helped the others craft it."

"You know my Destiny?" Christine asked, floored. What the hell?

Was that why the oracles proclaimed the Destiny of certain beings? Because the game was rigged, and they were the ones who had set the Destinies in the first place?

Toby gave an elaborate shrug, hands falling open to indicate his nonchalance. "I didn't set it," he said. "So I can't really say. That's one of the tricky things about Destinies. We craft them as carefully as we can, but what parts really take hold in a being is hard to say.

Sometimes the whole thing sticks. Other times, just pieces."

"Wow," Christine said. This was making so much more sense. Then she narrowed her eyes at Toby. "You're speaking really clearly for an oracle."

He sighed. "Yeah, that appears to be one of the side effects of moving between this plane and the others. Your memory of this may grow spotty. So I'll give you as clear a prophecy as I can; however, it isn't my fault if you don't remember all of it. You have been warned."

Toby's stature changed with the last words, and his voice grew deeper. Christine would swear that he'd suddenly grown in size as well, his chest filling out and broadening.

He also began to glow. The light hurt not only Christine's eyes but her soul.

Damn it! He wasn't about to turn into some awful angel, was he?

But no, that seemed to be the extent of his changes. He stood up, then kept growing, until he towered above them. The towel that he'd been wearing around his waist fell away, but at least the steam rose up to modestly cover him.

Christine just wasn't in the mood for a full frontal from some being of light. That might be enough to give her nightmares.

"Ask your questions," he intoned.

Light shone from his eyes like two beacons, the regular irises gone. It was pretty creepy, as though he was in the process of transforming into some damned lighthouse.

Christine found herself frozen into place. She couldn't

move or speak. Damn it! Was this just a side effect of the oracle transforming? Or some other spell?

Her magical elements inside of her seemed frozen as well. She could barely sense them, let alone touch or speak with them.

Maybe this was why the oracles insisted on talking with humans, as most humans were mundane.

Would Toby have talked with her if she'd brought her dad? She'd have to ask Laurie later.

After glancing at Christine, Dennis nodded and stepped forward.

They'd talked about the phrasing of the question that he needed to ask. Christine didn't know if oracles were like fairies or others of the *kith and kin* who delighted in taking things too literally—so if you asked for a million bucks, your living room was suddenly filled with male deer. Or if the oracles would twist the words to not actually answer the question you asked.

Having spoken a bit with Toby, Christine figured that as long as Dennis got across the gist of the question he was asking, they'd be okay.

Remembering the words the oracle said was going to be the difficulty.

"How do we end the Great War quickly?" Dennis asked. "Before it spills onto the human plane?"

They'd talked about stopping Lars, but while Christine suspected that was part of the solution, she needed to ask a more broad question. Perhaps stopping Lars wasn't the answer. Plus, they didn't necessarily need to imply that she was part of the solution. Maybe someone else needed to be fighting the final battle.

"You must assemble the obelisk of truth, and have your warriors pass before it," Toby intoned.

"How do we assemble the obelisk of truth?" Dennis asked quickly.

"The map is underground," Toby said. "It will lead you to the pieces."

Underground? What the hell? Christine would have gnashed her teeth if she could move. This was what she was talking about when it came to oracles. Why couldn't he give her a straight answer?

Where underground? And where were the pieces? And what was the price? And what the hell was an obelisk of truth? What did that look like?

She knew better than to hope that there might be a book somewhere that described such a marvel, or why it had been disassembled and its pieces scattered. Nobody wrote anything down. She was determined to change that general attitude when she could.

Before Dennis could ask another question, the steam billowed up in front of them. Christine found she could suddenly move. She took a deep breath and instantly started coughing, as if she'd just swallowed something wrong.

Christine bent over, her coughing fit continuing, even as she felt the heat that had been oppressing her bleed away. Suddenly, they were in the Bergen Place park again. Christine still stood bent over, coughing. Dennis stood beside her, his hand warm and solid on her back.

"You okay?" he asked, concerned.

The rest of the tour group were in the process of moving from the fossil tree to the next one. Probably less time had passed on the human plane than in that damned steam room.

"Quick," Christine said, clearing her throat again so she could speak clearly. "What was it the oracle said?"

Dennis blinked at her. "Oracle?" His eyes took on a distant look. "Something about truth," he said slowly.

"Obelisk of truth," Christine replied. "Help me remember," she said out loud, asking for her air power to capture her words. "Where is it?"

"Underground," Dennis said immediately.

Christine shook her head. No, that wasn't right. The obelisk wasn't underground. The pieces were, though.

Suddenly, Christine's air element spoke to her in a deep tone. No, wait, her air power had captured the oracle's words and was returning them to her.

She heard the deep tones again, telling her to assemble the obelisk. Pass the troops in front of it. And that the map was underground.

The words fled away as soon as Christine heard them.

"Damn it!" she said. She could only personally remember the obelisk of truth. Nothing else.

Why did the oracles have that effect? Was it just because that would make it too easy? Probably.

She couldn't remember anything of Toby either, except that he'd been a big dude, doing his best lighthouse imitation, light streaming from his eyes, ears, and mouth.

One of her powers—maybe water element—tried to tug on her attention. There was something else that Christine wasn't remembering.

Her water element gave her the shape of a regular man.

Had there been someone else there? And something about her Destiny?

But no matter how hard she tried, she just couldn't remember.

Oracles were just too damned slippery.

———

As the tour was finishing up, Ko San talked about the other tours that the Seattle Oracle company gave, such as tours of the Olympic statue garden, Capitol Hill architecture, as well as the Seattle underground tour.

Christine heard quiet gasps as Ko San listed the places. She felt her own head nodding.

Seemed as though the oracle had sent others on various quests as well.

Her own task would be to take the Seattle Underground tour.

As she came to that conclusion, her air power assured her that it would help.

Christine was particularly pissed off that she couldn't remember. However, at least she had a clue. The rest of these poor people didn't even have that.

After the tour finished, Christine nudged Dennis with an elbow. "Going to go ask Laurie for her phone number?" she said.

"Who?" Dennis asked, confused.

"Laurie," Christine said. "Little miss perfect?"

Dennis blinked at her, confused. "I don't know who you're talking about."

"You were all hot and bothered by the other tour guide

before we started," Christine said. She clearly remembered his attraction.

Dennis looked over at Laurie, standing next to Ko San, chatting easily. She carried the clipboard now, holding it tightly against her chest like a shield.

"Why would I be interested in her?" Dennis asked, clearly puzzled.

Christine didn't know what to say. "Okay, then."

"Come on, let's go. It's going to be an early morning far too soon," Dennis said, already walking away.

Christine glanced over her shoulder at Laurie, who was staring at Dennis, her expression somewhere between hungry and sad.

Sorry, Christine mouthed as she started walking away.

She wasn't about to tell Dennis that he'd been judged by Toby as not being good enough for his relative.

Then she, too, forgot all about the tour guides as they started walking back to Dennis's car and she began planning her next trip.

To take the Seattle Underground tour.

CHAPTER ELEVEN

"I'VE NEVER HEARD OF AN OBELISK OF TRUTH," NIK told Christine, well, truthfully.

She'd come by early that morning, talking to Nik as he stocked the shelves. As Christine was an occasional employee, he'd keyed the exterior portal to allow her access even if the shop wasn't open for business.

Nik had open boxes of charm bags on the front counter, and was counting the colors out before he refilled the shelves, keeping a close eye on the inventory. He'd already restocked the healing potions (including the huge gallon jugs), prayer flags (used to consecrate an army's staging area), and the barrels of ash (that the demons seemed intent on consuming.)

None of the posters lining the upper walls needed to be replaced that morning—he generally reserved that task for Mondays. The lights that shone down from the ceiling that morning seemed filtered, as if shining through thick canvas.

The lights in Nik's shop always reflected the desire of

the buyer, so that they could shop in the illumination they preferred.

Nik didn't like to think about what it meant that when he had this place to himself, the lights always reverted to the oldest setting possible, the one Nik remembered from the bad old days and the very first incarnation of his shop—the noon sunlight shining through a canvas tent.

"Damn," Christine said, shaking her head. "I'd at least hoped that you'd heard of it. I don't know what it is, or where to find it, or how to *assemble* it. Just that it's underground." She sighed and growled. "Why couldn't the damned oracle be more clear?"

Nik shrugged. He knew the oracle probably had spoken more clearly; however, it was one of their inherent traits that most couldn't remember the details of meeting one of them.

Even Nik had only vague memories of his own interactions with the oracles. He'd talked with one, once. Ages ago. Possibly back when he was still one hundred percent human, with a soul and everything.

But he could never remember the details, what the oracle had said, how Nik had reacted.

"What can you tell me about the oracles?" Christine asked after a moment. "And their damned quests?"

Nik gave her a smile. He hoped that she felt how warmly he intended it. "The oracles frequently give out quests or tasks for seekers. It's like the petitioners have to prove themselves worthy or something."

The eyeroll that Christine gave him was perfect in its extreme.

"In the oracles' defense, those who have been given a quest or a full Destiny rarely fulfill them," Nik said.

"Well, if I could only *remember* all the parts of it, I'm sure I could do it!" Christine growled.

"And I think that's part of it," Nik said. "I think they can't just tell people what they need to hear, or they'd negate free will. Or something."

Christine grimaced. "Free will and all that is great, if there are still people around to exercise it."

"Even if the demons win the Great War, there will still be people," Nik pointed out. "They won't be wiped out. The Host would never allow that."

"What if the Host has also been corrupted?" Christine asked.

Nik blinked. "Don't think that's possible," he said after a bit.

"Why not?" Christine said. "Isn't that what happened to start the races of demons in the first place? Angels who are fallen?"

Nik had no reply.

"And don't get me started on the Creator or God or the actual Devil. No one claims to have met either, not in the flesh. Angels and demons, sure. But the big guys are only ever talked about, never seen," Christine added hotly.

Nik nodded, considering his next words.

"Faith is an important tenant for the religions of the world," he said. "They all insist on believing in things that aren't provable, aren't seen."

Now, it was Christine's turn to shrug. "I'm not saying that the big guys are just a hoax run on the rest of us. But who are they? Really?"

Nik smiled. "I never expected to be talking with a princess troll about such things," he told her.

"A princess troll who is losing her war," Christine said quietly.

Nik's grin increased. "You'll be fine," Nik told her confidently. "You'll figure it out. You always do."

"And what if I don't this time?" Christine asked. She sounded so worried.

"Then humanity will spend a while at the bottom of the barrel," Nik said simply. "Sometimes, I don't think that would be the worst outcome possible. They might even learn some things as a result."

"So many would die, though," Christine said. "And there's no guarantee that they'd ever get back on top."

"They would," Nik said. "Though you doubt the existence of one of the *big guys* as you call them, I've seen enough of the shadows that they throw not to completely write them off. Sooner or later, the world would turn again."

"Thank you," Christine said.

"For what?" Nik asked. He hadn't been able to answer any of her questions. He couldn't give her true help, or else his precious neutrality would be called into question and he'd lose his immortal life.

"For giving me—not hope, but something to think about," Christine said. "Shadows to watch."

She nodded and left the shop, on to fight her next great battle.

Nik shivered slightly as he considered his shop. His pride and joy. The entire reason why he still lived and breathed, in a manner of speaking.

Nik's Emporium and Trade Goods. The only neutral territory for any of the wars, the great ones and the small ones. The place where every being could have a moment away from the battle lines, a safe place where they could breathe, just for a few moments.

He knew that he'd fulfilled a great service to many beings over the centuries.

But still…

Was his continued neutrality worth it? If the demons would really win?

Nik finished stocking the shelves but he didn't flip around the "open" sign as it were, didn't enable the portal for customers, not yet, though he could feel the presence of more than one on the other side.

Instead, he went into his back room. Above the workbench, he opened up a small pocket of space. It wasn't a normal spell. The pocket wouldn't travel anywhere with Nik. It was bound here, to this physical space. It wasn't impenetrable. But it was very, very, very difficult for anyone besides Nik to find or access.

Nik understood what the demons were doing with the pocket worlds that humans created, how they were corrupting and influencing them from the outside.

This pocket wasn't locatable by them, not using their normal methods.

And Nik intended to keep it that way.

He pulled out a small mirror on a stand from the pocket. A yellowed lace handkerchief covered the face of it. The stand looked antique, made of white porcelain with a delicate blue pattern painted on it. A solid gold bar rose from the base, then encircled the mirror itself.

Nik didn't remember when he'd acquired this piece. He sometimes felt as though he'd always had it. The piece had a tag on, written in a spindly script, declaring it the Mirror of Truth.

Nik had never understood why he'd hidden the mirror away. Some half-spoken truths that came to him in a dream, though Nik didn't truly sleep or dream anymore.

Or maybe the words had come from that oracle long, long ago.

Nik sighed and put the mirror back into the pocket and locked it up tightly.

If Christine came asking for it at the end of her quest, would giving it to her violate his neutrality?

Hopefully he'd have an answer to that question when the time came.

CHAPTER TWELVE

Lars bit back his impatience as he stewed outside Buddy's throne room. Though his appointment time had come and gone, he was still here, just *waiting*.

The hallway was just as old-fashioned as the throne room itself, filled with lava-spewing tiny volcanos placed in the most inconvenient locations, so that a demon, if he wasn't being careful, would be sure to either burn himself or ruin his clothes. The floor itself wasn't bad, just boring, plain cement with the occasional crack that burbled with hot tar. The walls looked as though they'd been carved out of rock by an impatient sculptor who'd just hacked out a space and hadn't bothered smoothing anything over.

Buddy had summoned Lars back down to Hell to supposedly celebrate his latest victory, or something. To be honest, Lars had barely scanned the invitation.

He'd only paid attention to the date and time—that he had to make an appearance today, now. Or, rather, seventeen minutes ago. And counting.

Lars took a deep breath and prepared himself to wait

some more. As long as it took. At least that homey sulfur smell soothed him, while not much else did. And he'd come down expecting to be forced to wait.

This was Hell, after all.

Although, being able to transform to his full demon body did feel good. A chance to stretch his wings, flex the leather between the tall, bone-like struts, feel the natural heat warm his belly scales. The acid that naturally dripped from his tongue tasted sweeter that morning. Perhaps a diet containing more raw meat—the flesh of his enemies—had helped with that.

He still had to be careful, though, to not brush against the irregular walls, certain that they'd been fashioned just to catch the unwary off guard and possibly damage one of his back or shoulder scales. And the spikes on his tail really needed some attention. Would have to find some minion to take care of that when he got back to the field.

On the one claw, Lars was pretty certain that at this time, with the way that things were going, he didn't really *need* Buddy anymore. Lars had more than enough recruits for his armies. The generals were obeying him and following his plans for the most part. And the money was pouring in, both through looting the *kith and kin* worlds after decimating the populations, as well as from the other demon princes wanting to make sure that their PR departments could claim alliance with the victor.

On the other claw, Buddy had been the first to believe in Lars, to see his brilliance. Even if it had taken a tortuous contract and what had seemed like endless negotiations to finally get those first armies.

The only part of the contract that hadn't been redlined

and rewritten numerous times was the one iron-clad, non-negotiable clause that specified that if Lars lost the Great War, Buddy would claim his soul.

While Lars knew that he was quite a catch, he didn't think that Buddy would sabotage the Great War just to capture Lars' soul. Or at least, not *merely* to do that. Even Lars didn't have that big of an ego. Most days.

Lars was more of a realist. Or maybe just a natural born politician.

He understood at a gut level that he needed to keep coming back to Hell on a regular basis to kiss Buddy's ass so that Buddy wouldn't have a real excuse to throw the Great War. Lars had to keep winning, and to keep up the appearance of winning, so that Buddy couldn't recruit other demons to work against Lars.

Even though it was in their best interests to work together so that they could win the Great War. Lars had no illusions about how the demon princes were all out for themselves and couldn't see beyond their own fiefdoms.

However, what Buddy didn't understand was that Lars had *plans* for him, too, after the Great War. How Lars would propose a house cleaning after he'd been unanimously voted in as a prince of Hell.

How Buddy might suddenly find his status reduced.

Of course, Buddy probably suspected this. You didn't become a prince of Hell by not understanding the threats around you. But even Buddy wouldn't suspect what was coming.

Plans within plans, wheels within wheels.

Finally, the door to the throne room opened and a herald motioned for Lars to come forward.

"The Supreme General, Lars Sorgenfreys!"

The herald's voice boomed across the…empty room?

Lars had expected there to be a party. The room should be filled with fawning supplicants. Hadn't the invitation mentioned a celebration?

Just Buddy was there, lounging on the throne at one end of the room, legs thrown over the arm, scratching his pot belly with long, yellow claws. The throne room hadn't changed—it still looked like a set from a B-rated Hollywood movie from the sixties, with all the rocks and lava and such. The throne, too, was such a throwback. Who sat on an iron throne made out of casts of your enemy's skulls?

This whole place needed spiffing up. Cleaning up.

Lars just had to bide his time.

"Supreme General, eh?" Buddy asked. He gave a loud belch. A flutter of smoke issued from between his flabby lips. The smell of burned tacos filled the room. "Then what should be my title?"

"Ah, excuse me?" Lars asked, confused.

That was part of the problem with demons. They all wanted to be generals. He'd had to invent a series of intermediate ranks, such as Squad General, not to be confused with Squadron General, Line General, Field General, Leader General, and so on, reserving the title Supreme General for himself.

"If you're the Supreme General," Buddy said slowly, "and I'm your superior, what should my title be?"

"Superior General?" Lars guessed.

"Ultimate," Buddy said with a grin. "You should call me Ultimate General."

"I'll have my people draw up the papers," Lars said immediately, though he had no intention of doing so. Ever. *Over my dead body.* Ultimate General indeed. Though he had to admit that he might have been a little pissed at himself for not having claimed the title first.

"So," Buddy said after a bit. "How goes the war? And you should use my title."

Lars managed to not grind his fangs together only by taking in another deep breath. And regretted it instantly. Seriously, the gas that Buddy passed could be used as a weapon. If Lars had been wearing his human body, he might be doubled over right now, coughing and choking.

"The war is going well…Ultimate General," Lars said. "It's all detailed in my reports."

Buddy waved a negligent hand. "Yeah, I know. I just wanted to hear it directly from the horse's mouth. You have had a lot of victories. What about the defeats?"

Lars shrugged as nonchalantly as he could with his wings folded tightly against his back. He didn't want to accidently trigger a cascade of nasty water from the waiting stalactites above.

"We lose individual battles now and again, that is true," he said.

Buddy looked at him with wide eyes, as if amazed that Lars would admit to any defeat.

"They don't matter in the overall scheme of things," Lars continued. "The number of small skirmishes that we lose is unimportant. What's important is that we're turning the tide in terms of the *kith and kin.*"

"Go on," Buddy said, nodding as if he understood, though Lars doubted he did.

"When I started the war," Lars said, unable to help the pride that filled his voice, "I knew that I had to change the alliances of the *kith and kin*. Traditionally, they've always aligned themselves with us. The intervening centuries with the humans at the top have weakened our ties."

"With you so far," Buddy said.

Huh. Most of the demons that Lars had tried to explain even this much to reacted either with confusion, or with demands to just tell the *kith and kin* that they needed to change.

Like that ever worked.

"So I needed to start killing the *kith and kin* races. Needed to show them that I was serious. I wouldn't negotiate any cease fires or withdrawals." Lars smiled at how well that had been working. "Now, not only are they falling all over themselves to align themselves with their proper masters, they've also starting to do our work for us."

"How so?" Buddy asked.

Wait, he'd actually followed that? Huh.

Maybe Buddy really was smarter than he looked.

"The Leafanders have now invaded the Boxilers," Lars said with glee. "While I might have *hinted* about that course of action, I didn't have to bribe them, pay them, or coerce them. They did it on their own."

Lars may have in fact been chortling about the attack since it had been first reported.

"Fascinating," Buddy said. He did look interested. "So what is the next step in your grand plan? Now that you've successfully picked off the easier targets?"

Lars scowled. The *kith and kin* worlds that he'd

conquered hadn't all been easy. But he didn't bother to correct Buddy.

Not yet.

"I will continue to attack *kith and kin* worlds at random," Lars said. He'd drawn up lists of places, then issued dice to his generals. They wouldn't know which plane they were attacking until after they'd rolled. "But I may, at this time, consider negotiations after an attack. As long as that particular world's inhabitants would both swear fealty, as well as seal the pact with blood—the blood of another *kith and kin* race."

"I see," Buddy said. He had a pensive look on his face. Was he actually hiding a scowl?

Didn't he understand just how brilliant Lars' plans were? Eventually, the demons would be able to withdraw while the battles between the *kith and kin* raged on.

And the demons could finally focus on their ultimate target: the humans.

Divide and conquer. A strategy as old as the rocks in this room.

"So who is leading the armies of the *kith and kin*?" Buddy finally asked after a moment.

Lars didn't growl. Not quite. Maybe just a soft grrrr. "That damned princess troll. Kizalynn."

"Weren't you originally sent to earth to keep an eye on her?" Buddy said. His tone sounded innocent enough.

Lars wasn't fooled.

"Yes," Lars said. "And yes, it was her testimony and trickery that sent me to prison in the first place. But don't worry. I have plans for her, too."

Buddy gave Lars a tight smile, his eyes narrowed. "You have plans for everyone, don't you?"

Though his tone was quiet, friendly even, Lars understood that he was suddenly in grave danger.

He had to remind himself that Buddy actually wasn't a fool, but a prince of Hell who had quite possibly earned the title.

"I'm not sure what you mean," Lars said, faltering.

But Buddy just nodded, as if Lars had answered his question in the positive.

"That's okay, Supreme General," Buddy said, still maintaining that quiet, menacing tone. "Your Ultimate General has plans for you as well. Thank you for indulging me with your presence this afternoon, catching me up on all your campaigns. We'll have to do this again."

"It—it would be my pleasure," Lars said, stumbling over his words.

Buddy waved his hand at Lars, dismissing him.

Lars gathered up his pride and marched to the door as if he didn't have a care in the world.

And he didn't. Not really. Buddy wouldn't stoop to stabbing him in the back.

At least, not yet.

Once outside in the hallway, Lars breathed a sigh of relief.

He saw his mistake now.

He'd assumed that the closer he got to victory, the easier it was going to be.

And in some ways, it would be.

However, it would also be the most dangerous time for him. He understood that now. Someone could assassinate him right at the end, make it look as though the enemy had gotten through to him. Or set some weird demon fraction up. If the plans were all in motion, and their win was guaranteed, Buddy and the other demon princes would no longer need Lars. They could kill him off, swoop in, and take all the credit for winning the Great War themselves.

Lars wasn't sure what he was going to do. But now that he saw the threat, he could plan for it.

He was good at that.

Feeling more assured, Lars continued on his way to the portal room to head back to the human plane, meet with his generals, direct his armies.

And generate even more complicated schemes.

CHAPTER THIRTEEN

"You know, I'd missed these," Ty admitted before he took another big bite of his burrito. It had the perfect proportions of spicy pork, refried black beans, cheese, and pineapple salsa. He was going to have to remember this place.

"Me too," Christine said with a grin.

After Christine had broken the changeling spell, before she'd started working at the fairy bridge, "Ty for lunch" had been a weekly occurrence for them. Ty would take Christine to one of the various *kith and kin* restaurants that he knew about, educating her about the various races of the *kith and kin* and the whole new world that had opened up for her. They'd tried to continue the tradition once she'd quit her day job, planning to meet once a month, but frequently they'd miss a month or three.

Then Ty had gotten injured, the war had started, and they hadn't seen each other much.

Today they were eating from a Mexican food truck downtown, with an all human staff, at least as far as either of them could tell. They were killing a little time before the Underground Seattle tour started.

They sat at the top of the Seattle Hill Climb stairs that led down to the streets and piers below. The sun had burned off the marine layer early, and the temperatures were heating up, soon to be oppressive. Cool winds blew up the stairs from the permanently shaded area below, scented with the smell of the water.

Tourists marched up and down the stairs, taking pictures all the while, gawking at the sights. A few businessmen and women took the stairs as well, those who knew how to find parking down below then walk up to their offices. Streams of joggers also paraded by, like colorful birds in their neon outfits and toned skin.

Christine had explained what they were looking for, at least as well as she'd been able to. She kept stumbling over her words, as if they were difficult to say.

Ty had seen this happen before. It came from being exposed to the oracles. Any super holy being, actually, tended to have the same effect. Angels had some control over it, particularly if they were making a proclamation. The oracles, it appeared, did not.

Or they did, and they were just assholes about it.

"Do you think the actual obelisk is underground?" Ty asked when Christine drew to an awkward halt.

She shook her head. "That would be too easy. I expect there's just another clue down there somewhere. It's going to be some sort of quest, I suspect." She sighed.

Ty waited while Christine composed her thoughts. It was something he appreciated about her. Though she was a troll, and her natural instinct was to rush right in, Christine retained a thoughtfulness about her.

"I can't ask you to take this quest for me," she said quietly. "But I can't be away from my armies for too long."

Ty nodded. He didn't ask how the war was going. Given Christine's general grim demeanor, he assumed that she was having the same success that he was searching for Lars.

Little to none.

He shared her belief that Lars was probably "hiding in plain sight" and living in his parent's house. But they'd never catch him there. He was too careful around that location. No, they'd have to surprise him out in the field. Ty had agents everywhere, searching.

And speaking of such…

A young executive came striding up the stairs. Possibly a lawyer, but definitely something powerful and white collar. His dark black skin practically shone with confidence. He kept his hair trimmed short, showing off the perfect features of his skull. The suit he wore cost more than Ty probably made over the course of half a year. It fit him impeccably across his broad shoulders, trimmed exactly right down to his waist. He carried a leather briefcase, handmade, of course, that matched his Italian leather shoes.

He paused as he came even with where they were sitting. He shook his wrist, showing the expensive silver wristwatch he wore there. "Excuse me, my watch seems to have stopped running this morning," he said. "Can you tell me what time it is?"

Even his voice sounded rich and powerful.

"Ten thirty," Ty lied.

Christine shot him a puzzled look, but she didn't say anything. It was actually closer to eleven thirty.

"Good," the man said. "I won't miss my lunch date with my wife at noon. Thank you."

He gave Ty a sharp nod then walked on.

"What was that all about?" Christine asked.

Ty gave her a big grin. He glanced casually around, making sure that no one was within listening distance. "That was a contact of mine. He was just checking in. Seems that he has a big meeting with some demons at noon. Trying to see if we can get the jump on Lars."

"Wow," Christine said, her eyes wide. "I had no idea."

"You have your own spy network, right?" Ty asked. He'd never really been in a war before. He wasn't quite sure how all of that worked.

"Yeah," Christine said. "But one of Ozlandia's people is in charge of it. I don't have to actually meet with contacts. I don't have time." She looked wistful for a moment. "I just have to fight."

"You're doing more than that," Ty assured her. He wasn't certain where all this self-doubt was coming from. Was Christine being influenced by demons? He didn't smell it on her, though he'd have to check again later.

Christine nodded. Ty didn't have to see her yawn to know how exhausted she was.

The war had changed her. Possibly not for the better, making her harder and more cruel.

They'd just have to see if she could break that spell too, and become someone else.

They finished their lunch in silence, each

contemplating the near future in their own ways—though neither of them had much hope.

Ty had never been on the Underground Seattle tour before. He'd been down in the sewers for the city—more times than he cared to remember, chasing one demon or another. He'd also gone careening through more than one alley, down fire escapes, over rooftops, and up so many staircases. (Somedays it seemed to him that the whole city was connected by stairs.)

He'd known about the great fire that had consumed most of the downtown area back in 1889. His people tended to be long lived (silver bullets and holy water not withstanding) so he had one grandfather who remembered the fire, though he'd been young at the time, not even a teenager.

Human history didn't much interest Ty, even though he was technically one half human.

He didn't perk up until they finally left the outdoor seating area of the bar where they'd gathered and finally approached the stairs to go underground.

The stairs were modern, of course. Metal and loud as they all trooped down them. Human built. Most of the crowds who passed through here were human as well. It had been a long time since any of the *kith and kin* had visited, at least as far as his nose could tell.

Ty took a sigh of relief when the cooler underground air struck his skin. He placed himself directly next to one of the tall black fans that were running. The concrete floors helped hold in the cooler air, as did the all brick walls.

The guide stepped up onto a wooden platform to address them, giving the history of where they were standing, the building that had originally been there.

He noticed that Christine wasn't standing beside him. She wasn't even paying attention to the guide, but had her back turned to the speaker.

What was she looking at? He craned his head forward.

Then the guide gestured to where Christine was standing, explaining the map of the underground that she was perusing.

That seemed to bring Christine out of her deep study. She started, looked around, then moved to the side so that others could also see the map.

Only then did she look over at Ty. She gestured with her head that he should join her. He nodded, showing that he understood. Then waited until the guide had finished her spiel and moved onto the next spot before he walked over to the map.

"Look closely," Christine said softly.

Ty looked at the map. It was cartoonish, showing the upper streets of Seattle with the underground original buildings directly underneath.

Wait. Were those buildings moving?

He blinked, trying to clear his eyes.

For a moment, a tall obelisk appeared in the center of the map. It appeared to be made of four pieces, though he couldn't quite catch the names. Just the bottom, which he thought it said something like "Vern's Vase."

Then the pieces flew apart. In the style of a National

Geographic video, each piece secreted itself in a different area of the map, the name of the location flashing briefly.

He turned to look at Christine, who nodded slowly at him.

The oracles had said that she needed to assemble the obelisk of truth.

Looked like it was going to be a treasure hunt.

———

At the end of the tour, Christine bought a copy of the map, then led them to a clear area of Pioneer Square where they could unfold it and look at it. A corner of the square had been set up with a two-piece band, a guitar player and a banjo player, singing original songs.

For a moment, Ty wondered if the main singer actually recognized Christine, given the way his eyes followed her. Ty raised his nose and sniffed. Yup. Guy wasn't fully human. He had black hair that fell into his eyes, a casual smile, and dark brown skin that spoke of a mixed family.

But then Christine gasped, and Ty forgot about Toby, the singer.

The obelisk was no longer in the center of the map that she held. The edges of the map were filled with ads from local stores. The center ad on the right side was a law firm that appeared to use an obelisk for their logo.

The map wavered again before Ty's eyes. The words "Vern's Vase" appeared beside the bottom of the obelisk that was the law firm's logo.

"Do you know where the Potichens live?" Christine asked.

Ty thought for a moment. "Yes," he said. "They're a peaceful race. Potters, actually. Their world doesn't have large land masses. It's mainly rivers. They collect the red clay from the banks to make their pots."

"And vases?" Christine said with a grin.

"And vases and cups and tiles and everything that they can," Ty said, nodding. "When do you want to go?"

Christine blinked, then pulled back from him. It was subtle, but Ty could see it in the way her shoulders straightened, the way she sat up straighter, as if preparing herself for a fight.

"I'm sorry," Christine said. "But I think…I don't think you're supposed to go with me."

Ty shrugged as if the words didn't sting. He's actually been looking forward to spending more time with Christine. Why didn't she want him to go along? Searching for demons was his specialty. He was really good at finding things. Was Christine pissed off because he hadn't found Lars yet?

"The piece is labeled as *Vern's Vase*," Christine explained. "I think I'm going to need to take my dad."

"Oh," Ty said. "That, that, actually makes sense." He looked down briefly, chagrined at his own lack of confidence.

"I don't want to put my dad into danger," Christine said. "He keeps asking what he can do for the war, and I keep putting him off. But it looks like I'm not going to have a choice."

"Vern has turned out to be a pretty powerful

magician," Ty pointed out. "Do you want backup? Do you want me to go anyway?"

Christine considered for a moment. "How about this. Can you set up the portal for us? And if we don't return after two hours, come to the rescue?"

"Done," Ty said. That actually sounded just fine to him. *Ty to the rescue.*

"Thanks," Christine said. She seemed relieved.

"It'll be fine," Ty assured her.

Christine pressed her lips together in a hard line for a moment before she finally said, "Magic has changed my dad. He doesn't seem to be the same person that I knew growing up."

"You're not the same person, either," Ty pointed out.

"True," Christine said. She thought for another moment before she shook her head. "Let's go get my dad," was all she said.

Ty nodded, but he heard the unspoken words anyway. He'd heard them often enough from Nik, himself.

Never trust a human.

CHAPTER FOURTEEN

"Wow. This is kind of groovy," Vern said, looking around the land of the Potichen in awe. He'd never been to a place like this. Heck, he'd never even imagined such a place.

First of all, the sky was yellow. Not the comforting yellow of sunflowers or buttercups. Nope, this was the amazing neon-yellow of a child's plush toy. Vern didn't get headaches, but he could see himself developing one if he had to spend a lot of time in this place.

Then there was the earth beneath his feet. While he saw a few dried weeds off in the distance, most of the ground was bare. Which wouldn't have been bad if the dirt had been a normal brown. Instead, it was all the color of baked red clay. And it smelled like clay too, that wet pottery smell, even though the ground was dry.

The problem was that the shade of yellow overtop and that shade of red clashed hard enough to set Vern's teeth on edge.

Christine must have felt the same way. He could hear a soft growl coming from her.

A blue river ran a few feet in front of them. At least it was a blue color found in nature, like in the Mediterranean on a sunny day, and not the chlorine blue of a pool. That might have been too much eye-searing color.

And Vern liked color. He considered himself a colorful kind of guy.

This was just too much.

Then there were the beings who inhabited this place, the Potichen, themselves. They were so tiny! The tips of the ears of some of the bigger ones may have come up to Vern's thigh. Their fur was almost the same color as the sky, that bright yellow, which on them at least looked cuddly. They looked kind of like rabbits, with black-tipped yellow ears sticking out of the top of their heads like antenna, a small pushed-out snout, and large buck teeth that gave them a slight beaverish look. They squatted beside the river bank on their solid hind legs while they worked the clay with their itty bitty fingers.

What was disturbing was how the clay tinted their fur, making their yellow hands appear blood stained.

No, that was not the most disturbing thing about the Potichen, Vern quickly discovered. The effect was much worse when they decided to lick their hands clean, staining the fur around their mouths red, making them look like blood-thirsty rabbits.

Christine continued her soft growl. His daughter was wearing her full troll body—something that Vern rarely saw. She normally wore an amalgamation of troll and human features around the family. She stood her full height beside him, close to eight feet tall.

She was dressed as a warrior. She had on ring mail, the rings sewn to a blue tunic, her muscled green arms bare. Her brown pants ended just below her knee, but tall black boots protected her shins. On her head, she wore a golden helmet, her tall pointed ears sticking out on the sides, making her look more menacing. Her huge, double-headed ax was still tied to her back, but Vern had the feeling that she could grab it at a moment's notice.

He felt positively underdressed for the occasion. It appeared that human magicians, at least the modern ones, didn't go in for long robes or capes. Honestly, he'd been a little disappointed when he'd learned that. Instead, he wore solid jeans and hiking boots, along with a nice looking, blue-striped button-down shirt.

What else were you supposed to wear when you went to work? Vern just wasn't sure. He'd thought about adding a vest, but that hadn't seemed cool enough. He would need to add something more to his outfit, though. Maybe a hat.

In his left, non-dominant hand, he did hold his wand. It had taken him a while to find the right one at Nik's shop. Too many had looked like children's toys to him, carved out of wood and all knobby, despite the power they may have held.

No, his wand was sleek, about a foot long, made out of a rod of dark blue resin with gold flecks swirling through the center of it. It didn't have an obvious tip, but Vern always knew which way to point it.

"You know what they look like?" Vern said, looking up at Christine.

"Like anime characters," she said with a growl. "Particularly with those eyes."

Vern didn't see what was so special about their eyes, until two of them looked up and spotted them. Their eyes grew comically huge, all white with tiny black pupils.

"When the Potichen are attacked, they generally flee rather than fight. Their magic allows them to disappear at will. See?" she said.

The two Potichen who had looked up and spotted them popped out of existence simultaneously, then reappeared just a few feet from where Vern and Christine were standing.

"They are vicious fighters when cornered," Christine added as the two beings, who appeared to be the greeting committee, approached them. "They also have a nasty electrical shock attack. Don't piss them off."

Vern nodded as he smiled at the two creatures slowly hopping their direction. He could totally handle this.

As his son was fond of saying, he was born ready.

"So's, I was sayin to my brother, here," Chunali said, continuing his explanation of how they'd founded this small town. "This is our home. Our digs. You got me?"

"Sure, I got you," Vern said, nodding earnestly. He felt both bewildered and amused. Particularly since it seemed as though the Potichen had learned English watching B grade movies and "Italian mobster" appeared to be the accent of choice.

The Potichen's homes were located in underground warrens, like rabbits. Christine had transformed the pair of them into miniature versions of themselves, though they both were much rounder, something to do with the conservation of mass. The four of them—Christine, Vern, and the two Potichen brothers—sat around a glowing bed of coals sunk into the center of their hosts' house.

The two brothers had insisted that they share a meal before they got "to the business of doing business with yas." The meal had mainly consisted of root vegetables braised in walnut oil and grilled over hot flames. It had been a little weird tasting with mint, cinnamon, and anise seasoning, but still delicious.

The room they sat in was round, with amazing tile on both the floor as well as the walls. The colors appeared random, yet they were done in a soothing pattern. Vern wasn't quite sure how they'd managed that. Maybe it was the way the colors flowed into each other, passing from paler versions into brighter colors and back again.

Now, one of their hosts was telling them of the clashes between the clans (which there appeared to be many) and how it was that they'd come to settle this area of their world, after escaping the heavy hand of the Mosetti brothers, the clan who lived just a couple miles away.

"It was a good thing you'd come to us," Kanuli continued, picking up his brother's story. "We can set you up."

"Yeah," Chunali said. "What he said."

They grinned at each other, two rabbits showing their

buck teeth and nodding their heads, their ears flopping like the cartoon characters they resembled.

Vern looked over at Christine, who gave him a firm nod. They'd discussed this before coming here: since it was his vase they were seeking, he should do the talking.

"We're on a quest from the oracles," Vern said when the two Potichen finally stopped mugging for each other and turned to their guests again.

"Oh, I gots ya," Chunali said. "Important stuff."

"Exactly," Vern said. "World saving, groovy stuff."

Vern could feel Christine practically pull something trying not to roll her eyes, while their hosts both oohed and ahhed at the implications, how their name would be tied to something so important.

"So whatcha need?" Kanuli said.

Vern hesitated. "A vase."

The two brothers looked at each other. The entire tenor of the room shifted abruptly, growing colder.

"What kind of vase?" Chunali said, throwing the words out like they were a challenge.

"I, ah, don't really know," Vern said. This had always been the problem. They didn't have a good idea of what this "vase" looked like, or how it became the base of an obelisk.

"We'll know it when we see it," Christine added.

"Well," Kanuli drawled after a moment. "I don't want to say we gots a problem here. We just might have to come to a different understanding though."

"I'm not following you," Vern said as the two Potichen stared at them.

"Us? We're tilers, *capiche*?" Chunali said. "We make

tile. We love tile. We live for tile. We make the most beautiful tile in all the worlds. No one, but no one, can compete with us when it comes to tile."

"Okay," Vern said slowly, still not understanding.

The brothers heaved a sigh in unison.

"Them other boys, the ones I was telling you about? The Mosetti brothers? They make vases," Kanuli finally explained.

"I see," Vern said. He glanced over at Christine, who shrugged.

Then Christine got a sly smile on her face.

"Wanna go on a raid?" she asked.

The brothers squealed in glee, thumping their feet on the tile floor.

Looked as though Vern was going to see the Potichen fight after all.

It amazed Vern how quickly Christine was able to organize the Potichen into squads. She knew exactly the right questions to ask about their attacks and defenses, splitting the groups up so there were both strong fighters and strong defenders in each.

When she was finished, they ended up with four squads with about ten fighters in each.

The plan was pretty basic. The brothers knew exactly where the warehouse of the Mosetti brothers was located. Since Christine and Vern couldn't just go and ask for a tour ("them Mosetti brothers are secretive that way") they'd just have to strike the warehouse itself.

Vern and Christine would sneak in from the back of the warehouse with two of the squads. For a diversion, the other two squads would strike the front of the warehouse, making it look more like a normal raid.

Once they found Vern's vase, they could "skedaddle out of town with the goods" before anyone was the wiser.

They would have to be outside the warehouse for Christine's portal magic to work, though. Seemed that the Mosetti warehouse, like the warehouses of all the clans, had special spells set into the walls that prevented any creature from just popping in or out.

As Christine was separating the fighters, Ty showed up. Seemed he'd been the rescue plan if Christine and Vern hadn't come back on their own accord after a couple of hours.

He agreed to sit this one out, as the Potichen all seemed deeply offended at him even being on their world.

Was that because he was part wolf? Was it their natural aversion to such a creature? But the brothers assured Christine that if Ty went with them, all their plans would be for nadda because everyone would be able to smell him and would come running to attack.

Finally, everyone was in place. Christine and Vern waited in an underground tunnel that rose up through the main floor of the Mosetti warren. It was just a few feet away from the warehouse itself. Kanuli was with them, waiting for word from his brother that the raid on the front had started.

The air was humid here, evidently closer to one of the rivers, or they'd altered one of the rivers to run through the warren, Vern wasn't quite sure. He put his hand on his daughter's shoulder, making her turn her head slowly, as if anticipating a threat.

"Just wanted you to know how proud I am of you," Vern said quietly. "The way you handled those fighters, getting everyone organized…You're really a marvel."

The smile on his daughter's face was startling. It made Vern realize just how infrequent those smiles had become.

"Thanks, Dad," she said. "I'm honestly looking forward to seeing you do your thing, too."

"Quiet!" Kanuli barked. He held his hand up to one ear, cupping it. Then he nodded.

"Show time!"

THE RUSH UP THE TUNNEL WAS EASY, AS WAS THE RUN to the warehouse. Christine easily brushed aside the guards standing there, knocking them out using just the side of her ax. Two of the fighters came forward. They carried a third fighter between them who was tightly rolled up, head tucked between the two hind legs, ears flat.

Then they flung the fighter at the door. He hit it hard, like a cannonball. As soon as he struck the wood, he discharged an electrical attack. The door splintered into a million pieces.

"Cool," Vern said appreciatively. Though he'd volunteered to blast the door himself, the brothers had quickly rejected his help—it needs to look like the usual setup, ya know?

Christine moved quickly through the gaping hole, using her ax to sheer off the remaining bits of wood clinging to the edges. She growled as she moved—well, waddled, really. The spell she'd used to compress herself had left her with short, stubby legs.

Vern wasn't much better himself. He'd always thought of himself as long and lean. It had taken a little time to get used to a body that was, quite frankly, pudgy. He carried his wand like a sword in front of him, ready to defend himself.

However, Christine quickly punched out the guards just inside the door.

Vern could tell that she'd almost used her ax on them. However, the brothers weren't actually looking for bloodshed. They didn't want this to escalate into an all-out feud. This was just a little payback.

All they really wanted was to help Vern acquire his vase.

Vern quickly raised his wand into the air and lit a magelight. It was a groovy glowing golden ball that followed him wherever he went.

If he'd been his normal size, the shelves probably wouldn't have come up to his waist. As it was, they reached almost to the ceiling, which was now far above his head. The shelves appeared to be made out of red-stained wood. Pottery lined every shelf. In the section they stood in, none of the pots, vases, or plates had been fired yet. They all held the same dull red color.

Vern realized that Christine, as well as everyone else, appeared to be staring at him.

"Which way?" Christine finally asked him, indicating the maze of shelves in front of them.

Vern gulped. He had no idea. He closed his eyes and waved his wand in front of him.

Nothing. Nada. No idea of where to go.

"This way," Vern said after a moment, leading them up an aisle to the right of center.

The only light came from Vern's magelight floating overhead. He heard curses and the muffled sound of breaking clay behind him.

As they neared what appeared to be the front of the warehouse, the pots grew more colorful. These were the ones that had been painted, and finally, the front area held the pots that had been glazed as well as fired.

Vern wanted to stop and admire the fine handiwork. The dishes, for the most part, were colorfully painted, the primary colors being reds and yellows, though some beautiful blues and greens were used as well. The plates held pictures of vegetables around the edges, while the vases were covered with flowers and vines.

"Here!" Kanuli said, calling them over to a different section.

Shelf upon shelf of vases confronted Vern. He quickly started walking between them, running his fingers along the edges, trying to get a feeling from one of the vases. Hell, he'd settle for a mere inkling at this point.

Nothing spoke to him.

Sure, the vases were pretty. Beautiful, even.

None of them struck Vern as being just the right level of groovy.

"Hurry!" Christine whispered urgently to him.

He heard the fighting now, just outside the door to his right.

"It's not here," he said after a moment.

"You sure?" Christine asked, fixing him with a hard stare.

Vern considered.

"Give me another couple minutes," he said. There might be something. Back in that far corner…

"You got it," Christine said. She took a fighting stance, her ax comfortably held in her hands. "I'll buy you as much time as you need."

"Thanks," Vern said, though he didn't like the look in his daughter's eyes. That was the troll, looking out at him. The one who didn't mind—might even enjoy—all the fighting and the killing.

Vern quickly went behind the shelf with all the vases, continuing his perusal. The vase had to be here. Somewhere. If only he had more time to think!

That had always been his concern. That there just wouldn't be time. If he just grabbed any vase and declared it as his, would that work? Possibly. Probably not, though.

He kept looking.

He heard the door to the warehouse splinter. He resisted the urge to go look, to join the fight.

He had a job to do. Find that vase.

Back Vern went, through the stacks. The sound of broken pottery followed him.

Along with the screams the Potichen evidently made when they were dying.

Just like rabbits.

Vern went around the last stack. There was a table up against the wall, also full of pottery.

These were not the fancy, professionally made items

that he'd seen earlier. No, it all looked like children's work. Maybe they were the product of a pottery class. The plates weren't symmetrical, the cups had lopsided handles, and the vases looked as though they'd fall over in a stiff breeze.

The glazing, also, was child's work. He recognized it from the finger paintings that his own children had brought home from school. All of the colors were as bright and brash as the sky, instead of the more subtle pairings of the adults.

Sitting on the corner of the table was a little blue lopsided vase. It had a raised swirl circling it, with dots here and there. Maybe they were supposed to be flowers on a vine?

Vern picked it up, studying it. It was about a foot tall and about as wide as his palm, not round but more oval in shape. The skin of the vase wasn't smooth. Like the blue glaze covering it, it felt blotchy. He could see the impression of the fingerprints of a little hand as it had tried to smooth out the clay.

The bottom of it appeared to have been signed—it had what looked like a C with a T tucked inside it, carved into the clay.

CT.

Christine Tuckerman.

His daughter, though he doubted that was the actual name that someone else was using.

However, someone's son or daughter had made this vase. It was important to some other father.

Vern was going to claim it as his own. For his own daughter.

And just pray that he'd chosen correctly.

VERN SHUDDERED AT THE SIGHT JUST BEYOND THE shelves. He held the little blue vase with one hand, pressed tightly against his chest. Christine had told him not to put it into a pocket world, on the off chance they wouldn't be able to get it out again.

Seemed as though the demons had ways around the pocket worlds that neither the humans or the *kith and kin* understood, so Christine wasn't taking any chances.

She wasn't taking any chances letting the Potichen through to him, either. He watched her swing her mighty ax like a baseball bat, taking off the head of her nearest attacker while flinging the body far.

The screams. He'd never forget the screams. Or the smell, either, worse than the sour bodies of the homeless or the rotting marshes next to Lake Washington.

Or how his daughter appeared to growl with delight when another creature dared to attack her.

She'd been right, the Potichen were fearsome fighters.

However, they were up against someone who was much, much more deadly.

The electrical attacks they threw at her bounced off a magical shield she maintained. The Potichen who got too close were frequently swept away by her winds. The ones that got through, she slaughtered.

"I have it!" Vern loudly declared, just to get Christine to stop killing the little yellow rabbits.

Though Christine didn't turn to look at Vern, she did nod once to indicate that she'd heard him.

From the side, one of the initial squads of fighters that

Christine had assembled suddenly formed up and came rushing out into the melee.

The fighters defending their warehouse were caught off guard. They turned away from Christine toward the other, more accessible, fight.

"This way!" Kanuli shouted.

Using both her hands, Christine shot out a hard wind, bowling over friend and foe alike, giving them a few moment's breathing room. Then she turned and raced toward Kanuli.

Vern followed, trying not to be too squeamish about stepping in bright red puddles of blood or over fallen plush toys.

They quickly made their way out the back of the warehouse. The squad of fighters there still stood just inside the door, ready and able to get them out.

As soon as they pressed through the broken door, Christine stopped, slapped her ax onto her back, then sketched a doorway in the air with both her hands. A blue, shimmering light sprang up, outlining the portal.

"Thank you," Vern said to Kanuli bowing his head.

"You get the goods?" Kanuli asked.

Vern held out the pot he'd acquired, showing it off proudly.

Kanuli looked puzzled, and scratched the back of his neck with a red-stained paw. This time, it was blood that colored his bright yellow fur, and not clay. "Youse sure that's the one?"

"It's a piece that would make any father proud," Vern explained. He stayed where he was instead of leaving through the portal, even though Christine was urgently gesturing for him to go through.

It was important that the Potichen understand what they'd sacrificed so many lives for.

"Oh," Kanuli said after a moment. "A father's pride." He gave a bright smile. "Something that warms the heart. Nice."

"Come on," Christine said, her tone starting to sound frantic.

"Thank you," Vern said before he turned and hurried through the portal.

He stepped directly into the living room of Christine's underground house. Christine came through behind him.

Vern rolled his head, stretching upward, finding himself back at his normal height and proportions.

Without pause, Christine turned and sketched another portal. Instead of going through herself, she threw what looked like a green rock through the opening. Then she closed the second portal.

"That will let Ty know we made it out safely," she said.

She turned to study Vern. She still wore her full troll body, with her muscled chest, stout legs, upper and lower tusks. Scratches ran down her arms, and blood stained her hands as well as her outfit. She didn't seem winded after the fight or even bothered by it.

Chances were, she'd seen, and done, much worse.

"Let me see it," Christine said after a moment.

He held out the vase to her. It looked like a child's toy in her large palm.

"You sure that's the right piece?" she asked Vern, skeptical.

"Look at the bottom," he directed.

She turned it over and grunted. "CT?" she guessed after a moment.

"A father's pride and joy," Vern said simply.

Christine blinked. She shrank down suddenly, flowing into a more human shape and size.

Was she crying?

"Thank you," she said softly as she handed the vase back. She caught his hand in one of hers and squeezed it.

"Can I get a hug?" she asked, her voice sounding much younger.

"Always, darling," Vern said, though he appreciated being asked as he now understood his daughter's reticence when it came to physical touch.

He wrapped his arms around his daughter and pulled her to his chest, sighing.

He knew he couldn't protect her. He couldn't wrap her in cotton and keep the world away. He couldn't take away the sights she'd seen, the blood she'd spilt.

But maybe, just maybe, he could help her live with what she'd done, get past the war and beyond.

She was, after all, still his little girl, whom he was so proud of it made his heart hurt.

CHAPTER FIFTEEN

TINA WOKE UP FEELING GOOD.

It was amazing how every day seemed to be different. There were mornings, okay, so most mornings, when she woke up and even though she was in her childhood room, it felt like a dungeon that she needed to escape. No matter how bright the sunlight was coming around the edges of the blinds on the window, it still felt like a dark, dank cave.

But that morning, the room looked…normal. Her bed was snug up against the far corner, the walls strong and safe. She'd painted the room a soft peach color over a decade ago, when she'd been eighteen. The color had faded, but it still made her smile. She might have to repaint one of these days.

The white woodwork around the windows and the doors stood out brightly, giving the room a clean look. Surprisingly, the floor didn't have piles of clothes on it or stacks of dirty dishes. Then she remembered. She'd felt good last night as well, and had cleaned her room. She looked out on the expanse of soft gray carpet. She'd even vacuumed, so it wouldn't be crunchy when she walked on it with her bare feet.

Tina took a deep breath. The smell of toast and coffee had snuck in from the kitchen downstairs. It didn't immediately fill her with distaste, but instead made her think that maybe she could eat something that wasn't sugary and disgusting.

Gingerly, Tina slid to the side of the bed, touching her toes down on the ground.

Her good mood held even as she pushed herself off the bed and onto her own two feet.

She tugged down the T-shirt she was wearing and looked around. Her eyes rested for a moment on the new wand that her adoptive parents had bought for her, which still sat, waiting for her, in a glass box on top of the wooden desk in the corner.

It didn't hurt to look at it. That was an improvement. She knew that.

They didn't have to know that she'd snatched her old wand from the townhouse the first day she'd been sent here, keeping it safe in a pocket space.

She hadn't been using it. Not yet. The magic still hurt too much.

But today was a good day. She resented how long it had taken her to get to this point. How much work and effort and damned stinky baths she'd had to take to wash away the corruption spells that had been placed on her. How hard it was rid herself of the demonic influence.

It was all Christine's fault.

If only Christine hadn't broken the changeling spell!

Then Tina would have retained her Destiny. The demons wouldn't have been able to get to her like they had. Her own Destiny would have protected her.

Sometimes she recognized that she was being illogical. The demons had captured her once, intent on twisting her Destiny.

This morning, and it was a good morning, she knew the truth.

If it hadn't been for Christine, Tina would still be one of the most powerful human magicians around. It would be *her* leading the troops against the demons. Not her troll sister.

Tina sighed. Then she took a deep breath, raised her hands, and pushed the air out loudly, while releasing the negative energy.

It was still a good day. She was finally starting to regain her strength. Soon, she'd be able to use magic again. It would come back, or so her teachers assured her every time they met.

The magic would come easily again, would surround her and fill her and be like breathing.

Then, and only then, would she meet with Christine again.

And get her vengeance.

CHAPTER SIXTEEN

KING GARETHEN DIDN'T WANT TO MEET WITH MANNY the cambion. However, the demon had been most insistent, actually threatening to come and visit the king when he held open court. So he'd finally agreed to a meeting that night.

Not that the guard would have allowed Manny into the court. No matter what the cambion might say, the guard wouldn't believe that he'd struck a deal with the king.

Were all his guards above being bribed by those shiny trunks of gold that the cambion gave out with abandon? King Garethen believed that his guard were honest, for the most part. He'd cleaned out the bad elements.

However, he didn't want them tempted, either.

The king, himself, had never accepted a bribe. No, he was just helping his neighbors out of a bad situation. They paid him out of gratitude. Nothing more.

Instead of meeting at the palace, the king arranged for a night out for himself. He didn't do it often, particularly now that the war had started. But he sometimes disguised himself enough so that no one would know who he was and he went into the city to indulge himself in some harmless drink, listening to the merchants and common, good trolls.

Kizalynn had shown the king how to better his disguise. So he now appeared to have a just a fringe of white hair trimmed shortly around his neck, instead of the full head of long hair he normally wore. He felt it made him look older and more distinguished. He'd toned down the green in his skin, making it similar to the earth color of most of the farmers. Gold caps now covered the ends of his two lower tusks, decorative but not useful. Wouldn't stand up in battle. He kept the top of his right ear lopped off—that had proven to be the most difficult part of his disguise to maintain.

He wore a common-looking white shirt, with long sleeves that tied at the wrists, a fashion popular among the well-to-do merchants, instead of the sleeveless tunics of the warriors that showed off their scars as well as their muscles. His pants were plain gray wool cropped just below his knee, with sturdy sandals that everyone seemed to be wearing, which had actually proven to be quite comfortable.

At his waist, Garethen still kept a good knife, tucked into a finely made black leather belt. He'd never mastered the human trick of pockets of space in which to tuck more weapons. He couldn't hide his ax someplace nearby, either. He considered himself a good enough fighter, however, that he would be able to give as good as he got in any brawl.

Not that he was looking for a fight. As much as he might want to join his troops on the battleground, he left the war and much of the day-to-day fighting to his adopted heir.

He'd thought, more than once, about calling her to the safety of the palace, making her direct more of her armies from a safe distance. However, that wasn't the custom of any troll. By proving herself in battle, the rest of the trolls would be more than willing to follow her when it was time for him to abdicate the crown.

At his heir's insistence, King Garethen did always leave a note about going out for the night so that no one would suspect he'd been kidnapped. He made sure to emphasize that he was leaving of his own free will.

And he always mentioned that Kizalynn was still his heir so that the guards wouldn't try something foolish like backing some idiot from the court who decided to take over instead.

The guard was faithful to him.

Manny had suggested a tavern that the king had never visited before. It was a little too close to the tanneries for the king's taste, as the stench of the vats of excrement and urine used to soften hides hung in the air. The buildings here were poor, made out of rough-hewn wood instead of solid brick or stone.

The darkness of the street didn't bother Garethen—all trolls had excellent night vision, which came in handy when you were working in tunnels. The way the buildings lurched in close to the street, seeming to loom above it, did make him uneasy, as if he walked in a jungle beneath trees full of predators.

Light spilled out from the open tavern door, along with the sound of a boisterous crowd. It gladdened King Garethen's heart to hear such gaiety. Too often the mood of everyone he met with these days seemed somber.

Or maybe he was just too used to his meetings with the treasurer, who continued to predict dire outcomes for the king's vault, or Ozlandia, the head of the guard, who also only ever had bad news.

With a lighter heart, King Garethen stepped into the tavern. Though the walls were wood, the floor was solid earth underneath.

Lamps hung from every corner, as well as from long ropes strung across the ceiling, so the room seemed as brightly lit as day. To his left, a group of trolls cheered as one of their members scored a bullseye in the game of blind darts they were playing.

Generally, a troll could hit anything he or she threw at. It was why, as part of the traditional uniform of the guard, they had a string bag full of sharp rocks hanging from their belts.

In blind darts, the challengers were blindfolded, then spun around several times. It made for a fun party game, particularly if the contestants had been drinking.

In addition to being able to hit anything they aimed at, trolls also generally knew which direction they faced, another useful trait when working underground and not having any obvious landmarks.

However, the combination of drink, spinning, as well as being blindfolded, would confuse most trolls. It was why the entire wall behind the dartboard was full of holes from where darts had widely missed the mark.

Garethen wouldn't be surprised if more than one troll in the crowd had also been struck by an errant throw.

Maybe later, after his meeting, Garethen would have to see if he could join the game.

Before Garethen could take another step into the crowd, his nose told him that not all of the beings here were trolls.

In fact, the crowd appeared to be mixed.

Unusual.

Garethen didn't stare, or try to determine what other sort of beings were in the room, not until he got to the front of the room.

Kizalynn had taken him to a human bar once. He hadn't enjoyed it, despite the number of good stouts and hoppy beers he'd tried that night. Seemed that humans enjoyed a lot of different types of alcohol and had rows of bottles filled with liquor behind the bars there.

Here, two solid kegs were stashed behind the counter where the barkeep stood. Each was about five feet in diameter and probably five feet long. The one on the left had a dark charcoal mark just above the wooden tap. The other was unmarked. Garethen assumed that meant that one of the beers was darker than the other.

That was much more sensible. So many choices of beers and hops and flavors had just confused him. Dark or light. That was all the choice he needed.

"Dark," he told the barkeep when he finally got her attention.

"Three pieces," she told him as she snagged a solid wooden mug.

Garethen knew better than to protest. He might have tried bargaining—surely the beer only cost half that.

But he wasn't a local. No one here could vouch for him. He was going to pay tourist prices, at least until the third or fourth round.

Only after reluctantly paying the exorbitant fee for the beer (and really, the beer wasn't worth it, though it did have a smooth, chocolatey aftertaste) did Garethen look around the room.

No tables or booths lined the edges of the room, which surprised Garethen. Not because it was unusual, but where the heck did the cambion expect to meet him in this noisy, crowded space?

There weren't any humans here, which made him breathe a sigh of relief. He understood that while Kizalynn was a changeling, and had grown up around them, Garethen just couldn't be comfortable around them. They all seemed too whiny. Plus, you could never trust a human. They might turn on you at any time.

There were a few orcs there, tucked into one of the far corners. They appeared to be haggling hard with a troll merchant. There were also a couple of the bright folk, half-elves or something, who harmonized a quiet ballad with two surprisingly good troll voices.

Then there were the demons. That was the smell that had struck Garethen first.

Why were there demons here, in Trollville? What were they doing?

That wasn't right.

Garethen was about to put his beer down and go to

fetch the king's guard when a hearty voice called out to him. "Yonarik! Over here!"

It took Garethen a moment to remember the name he'd chosen to travel under that night. He turned and spied Manny standing close to the door.

Garethen's nostril's flared. That was where the smell of the demons was coming from. It was Manny and his friend.

The king himself was why there were demons out that night.

A heavy hand fell on his shoulder. "They friends of yours?" the barkeep's low growl sounded from behind him.

"Acquaintances, only," Garethen assured her.

"Find another place to meet next time," she told him firmly. "I try to serve all types here, and keep the king's peace, but they're pushing their luck."

"I'll let them know," Garethen told her.

"Yonarik!" Manny said as Garethen came up. "So good to see you!"

At least the demon hesitated and didn't give Garethen a hardy slap on the back, though it appeared that Manny wanted to.

The demon had done an adequate job on his own disguise. His skull was still mostly bare, with mere patches of greasy hair growing out of it. But he'd shrunk his nose down to more human proportions, though it still dripped yellow snot. He'd hidden his eyes as well, making the color lighter, to that of a cloudy night instead of the stuff of nightmares. His hands bore six fingers, with shorter claws, and sandals covered his four-toed feet.

His companion, if Garethen had to guess, was

probably a cambion as well. He also had a vaguely human appearance. Seriously ugly human, with oversized, rotting teeth, warts, and dirt encrusted creases on his neck and arms.

Manny introduced his "cousin" Jack. Garethen nodded politely in his direction, but didn't bother to shake hands.

He'd already have to take a long, hot soak in order to remove the odor of the room, as well as wash away the presence of the demon.

"What did you want to talk with me about?" Garethen asked, cutting directly to the chase. No matter how nice the beer might be (and, all right, he was starting to enjoy it more) and how delightful it had been sneaking out of the palace (and no one believed that trolls could be sneaky!) he still wanted to cut down the time he spent with demons.

"We thought we could maybe do some more work with you," Manny said. He seemed taken aback at how the king was responding.

Had he really believed that the king would just come out drinking with him? They had strictly a business deal. Nothing more.

"And?" the king said when Manny didn't continue.

"We've got some good equipment for sale," Jack said. "Sturdy."

"What sort of equipment?" Garethen asked warily.

"Swords. Axes. Helmets. Like that," Jack replied. "We're willing to sell it to ya cheap."

"New?" Garethen asked. The war was, actually, costing

him a lot in terms of equipment, making sure that his troops had the best.

His guard still seemed to resent the refurbished swords and axes that he sent to them. Stupid superstition that if an ax had failed once, it would do so again, even if it was merely the handle that broke and the metal head was still fine.

"Barely used," Jack assured him. "Like new."

"You know that I'm outfitting troll armies, right? The weapons I need must be crafted specifically for trolls," Garethen said emphatically, figuring that would derail the conversation quickly.

Demons only made equipment for demons, right? Not for trolls.

"These are!" Manny told him. "Troll made, for trolls."

"Where did you get them?" the king asked warily. Were the demons coming in and stealing weapons from his blacksmiths? He'd have to set up extra guards and wards around the smithies and storage rooms, just in case.

"Oh, here and there," Jack said. "Amazing what you can find if you keep your eyes open. Always looking for the right opportunity."

"Where do you keep these weapons?" King Garethen asked. It wouldn't hurt to look, right?

He didn't like the smile the two demons exchanged. This wasn't a trap, right? They wouldn't be stupid enough to actually try to kidnap the king of the trolls?

Besides, there was no telling what Christine would do if they actually killed him. She might decide to storm Hell itself for him.

He gave them a cold, cruel smile in return, suddenly confident where he stood.

The demons looked puzzled, as they should. They thought they had him over a barrel. Ha!

"Let's go, boys," King Garethen said. "Oh, and we're never meeting in public like this again," he added before he turned away, placing his mug on the counter.

He caught the barkeep's eye and gave her a nod, letting her know that the demons wouldn't be returning.

Though he might.

That had turned out to be really good beer.

———

THE TWO DEMONS LED KING GARETHEN TO A DARK alley, just a block away from the tavern. The smell of the tanneries was stronger here. Without thinking about it, King Garethen called up a good stiff breeze to blow the scent away from them.

What good were magical powers if you couldn't use them sometimes to make yourself more comfortable?

The demons didn't seem to notice the smell. Figured. They were probably used to such a stench.

When had Garethen decided to get so friendly with demons? It was this war. Once it was over, he could cut all ties to the cambion. Never have to see Manny again. Even if that meant fewer trunks of gold in his private vault.

It didn't surprise Garethen that Manny pulled out the first weapon from a pocket of space. The humans had perfected that trick and the cambion were supposedly half human.

The sword the demon pulled out was good quality troll work. No nicks or scratches on the blade. It had a nice heft to it as well.

"Where did you say you got these?" King Garethen asked as he sighted down the blade. His troops really would be happy with such a weapon. As long as they didn't know where it came from.

"Here and there," Jack insisted.

That answer still set Garethen's back up. Yet, it was a high quality blade.

"What else do you have?" he asked, handing the weapon back.

Even in the dark he could see Manny grin.

Stupid demon had never bargained with a troll before. Ha! He'd learn quickly that he wasn't going to get the better end of this deal.

Manny pulled out an ax this time. The haft had been broken, but the blade itself was newish. There was a single long scratch on one side.

Garethen sniffed the broken end of the handle. It smelled mostly of demon, but there was a hint of troll underneath. Not only had the ax been made by a troll, for a troll, it had been wielded by a troll at one point. He put the ax down next to his feet, his unease growing. "What else?"

Manny pulled out two more axes, along with another sword.

King Garethen reached for the sword. While his hand remained steady, he felt his insides quaver.

This sword had belonged to one of the king's guard.

Bile filled the back of his throat.

He suddenly knew where "here and there" was.

The demons were trying to sell his own equipment back to him. The equipment of trolls who had fallen in the war.

"How dare you?" King Garethen roared. He wildly swung the sword at the pair of cambions.

The demons had been expecting his reaction, however, as they both had already moved out of the way.

The king didn't try to attack again. Though he was certain he could take them if it came to that, he didn't want to have to explain how he'd met up with them in the first place.

"Why on good earth did you think that I wouldn't recognize what you were doing?" Garethen growled at them.

"We counted on you figuring it out," Jack said. Manny nodded.

"Then why did you think you could just sell them to me?" Garethen asked, confused.

Suddenly, four more demons materialized out of the darkness. "We knew you'd require some persuasion," Manny added.

The king gulped. Two demons he could easily take. Probably three as well. Four was more iffy.

Six? He wasn't a young troll anymore.

"But why?" the king asked. What was the full plan of the demons?

Manny shrugged. "We actually need another favor. More passage through Trollville. We got a lot of refugees coming through, now that the war's started."

"And in exchange, we'll give you all the weapons we grab," Jack assured the king.

"All of them?" the king asked, running his finger along the cool edge of the blade. It was fine work. Maybe he could say the weapons came from his own team who'd scoured the battlegrounds after each conflict.

It was technically true, after all. He just didn't have to say that the team was composed of demons.

And to get all those weapons, and not have to pay any more gold for them…

"Just cambions, right?" King Garethen said, wavering.

Jack and Manny looked at each other. The four other demons melted away into the darkness again.

"Mostly, yes," Manny said after a moment.

"Just cambions," King Garethen insisted.

The two demons sighed, like a merchant conceding a point. "Fine. Mixed human demons," Manny agreed. "Cambions."

"Then I agree," the king promised. Funny, that ringing tone that echoed after his words, deep in the earth where such promises were recorded, sounded a little tinny this time.

King Garethen gathered up all the weapons that the demons handed him and marched back to the palace. He was looking forward to surprising the blacksmiths in the morning with his haul. They'd be able to clean and refurbish everything, put them into the waiting hands of his fighters.

And not have to spend a single piece of gold.

CHAPTER SEVENTEEN

DENNIS COULDN'T HELP BUT BE PUFFED UP WITH pride.

Not only had Christine been relying on him for recruiting, now she actually wanted him to go fight with her!

He'd actually had a T-shirt made up for when this day came. *I was born ready* was proclaimed in big, bold, white letters across a black background.

Christine just rolled her eyes when she saw it. "Here," she said, handing him a boring, off-white vest that had rings sewn into it. "Put this on."

Dennis pouted. He'd been expecting to show all the worlds his readiness. At least Christine let him keep his own jeans and heavy hiking boots.

They stood in the living room of her underground warren. While the ceilings were high enough for a troll and there were colorful Christmas-tree-like lights stretched across where the ceiling met walls, it still gave Dennis the feeling of being too closed in. In many ways, it resembled

Christine's old apartment, with books piled everywhere, a comfy chair in the corner with a light perfectly perched over the back of it for reading, as well as a large couch for napping on.

The walls were made out of smoothed-over rock, with some pretty stones left *in situ*. The ground, though, was just packed dirt. He'd never been able to talk Christine into getting some rugs, despite the fact that he still thought she needed just a touch of something to make this place homey.

She claimed it was plenty homey for her, reinforcing once again that the sister he'd grown up with technically no longer existed.

Next, Christine handed Dennis what felt like a metal-reinforced motorcycle helmet. It was a dark blue color. If only she'd handed him everything the night before! He could have put cool racing decals along the sides of the helmet and maybe a mohawk of purple fringe.

He lifted the helmet, feeling its weight. Damn, that was going to be a pain in the ass to wear.

She merely nodded at him. "You can just carry it for now and put it on later."

With a grin, Dennis tucked the helmet under his arm. Then he looked expectantly at her. "Where's my weapon?"

Christine merely snorted at him. She was dressed in a similar vest to his, though her ring mail was sewn to a dark blue vest, leaving her arms bare. A gold helmet perched on top of her head, with room on the sides for her tall troll ears. Her great ax was attached to her back, a short sword hung on one side of her belt, and a bag full of sharp rocks on the other side. She had knives sticking out of the tops of her black boots as well, below her cropped pants.

"What, I don't get a weapon?" Dennis asked, a little hurt.

"You're already armed," Christine said.

Dennis looked at her, confused.

"You can talk your way out of anything," Christine said. "You don't need the weapon. The armor is just to protect you until we can get to the point of talking."

"Oh," Dennis said, only slightly mollified.

"Look, the beings that we're going to see don't like trolls. They don't much care for humans, either. And we need them to help us," Christine said. "I'm not bringing an army to fetch what we need. I have you. That should be enough."

"Thanks," Dennis said, though he wasn't convinced Christine meant it as a compliment.

"You're my brother," Christine told him. "I've already lost too damned many good trolls and other beings to this war. I'm not about to lose family, too."

"Then why not bring an army?" Dennis asked.

Christine sighed. "I'm hoping that if it's just the pair of us, we can sneak in, grab what we need, and sneak out again, without them being any wiser. However, since plans never work out in reality, I need to be prepared for fighting as well."

"But we have no idea what exactly we need, right?" Dennis asked. "I mean, beyond the Torso of Dennis." He had to grin at that. Again.

Him, being part of the quest for obelisk of truth. Contributing his part. As long as they didn't expect him to actually hand over his torso. He was kind of using that already.

"Yeah. Vern's vase. Your torso," Christine said. "Once we had the vase, the next part showed up on the map. So I won't know what I'm looking for next until after we return. With the torso." She grimaced. "Dad's vase doesn't look like much. It wouldn't have been the vase that I would have chosen. So keep an open mind about what the map actually means by a torso."

"Got it," Dennis said. He grinned up at her. "Let's do this."

Christine sighed again, but she sketched the outline of a door with her hands. A blue light sprang up.

His sister really had gotten a good handle on all that magic stuff.

For a moment, Dennis had a twinge of regret that Dad had been the one who'd turned out to have magic and not him.

Then he squared his shoulders. It was okay. He had other talents, other gifts.

His sister, and the war, were depending on him.

He could do this.

He was, after all, born ready.

Dennis regretted not bringing an oxygen mask or something as soon as they stepped out onto the rocky hillside. He couldn't help but start coughing immediately. His eyes began watering as well.

"Crap," he heard Christine mutter next to him as he bent over, continuing to cough.

A warm wind suddenly caressed his face, blowing away much of the stink of sulfur and rotten eggs. He straightened up, wiping the tears from his eyes with the back of his hand.

The wind continued, blowing constantly, as if a tiny, invisible fan had been set up just a few inches in front of his face.

He looked over at Christine, who just shrugged. "Sorry," she said. "I knew this place stank. I came here once with Ty, just so I could create my own portal here. Didn't know it would hit you so hard."

"That's okay," Dennis said. "Thank you for the wind." He realized that it was her air power that was protecting him from the smell.

Kind of handy sometimes, having a magical sister.

He looked around. They stood on a desolate hillside. Bleached white rocks tumbled down the slope. Large boulders, as big as two cars stacked on top of one another, stood on either side of a wide trail leading back up the hill. A searing blue sky with a bright sun glared at them.

"So where are we?" Dennis asked as Christine turned around, looking in all directions.

"We're on one of the sacred hills of the Longians," Christine told him.

"Sacred?" Dennis said. Crap. Were they about to desecrate a holy place? Probably already had, just by being here.

While Dennis hadn't always believed in God or the Devil, he certainly had changed his tune after meeting an angel. As well as getting into a couple of scraps with demons. All of the *kith and kin* had some sort of creation myth and believed in a Creator if not the human God.

Dennis had participated in more than one prayer session, particularly fervent when whatever beings were about to engage in one of their sports. It had, but hadn't, surprised Dennis that the *kith and kin* prayed more before a game than before battle.

Battle was merely life or death. While a game was about eternal pride and bragging rights.

"The Longians have no towns or physical structures," Christine told him. "No workshops or houses. They either sleep on the rocks or in the air."

Dennis nodded. Christine had told him about the beings they were visiting. They most closely resembled a Chinese dragon, except that they had four sets of hands along their long bodies, a more pug-like face, and they tended to have iron spikes that ran down their spines to the ends of their long tails. Which appeared to be prehensile, at least as far as Christine could tell.

It still offended the librarian who lived at the heart of his sister that there were no books about the various races, no handy guide to the *kith and kin*. He suspected that once the war was over, she might write one. Just for her own reference if no one else valued such a thing.

"The only place I could find where they might gather, or, you know, have a torso lying around, was in their sacred caves," Christine continued. "But I wasn't able to sneak into one earlier. I'm just hoping we can find something there. Unless you think that there's a better place we should go? Now that we're here? Does any direction feel more appropriate than another?"

Dennis shrugged. He didn't feel drawn to one place more than another.

"Close your eyes," Christine suggested. "See if you can feel something."

Dennis obeyed, closing his eyes for a moment and seeing if he felt something tugging him one direction or another.

"Nothing," he announced after a moment.

"Then let's try the caves," Christine said. She reached behind her. Her ax leaped off her back and into her hand.

"Pretty neat trick," Dennis commented.

"Huh?" Christine asked. Then she gave him a shy smile. "Thanks," she said. "Took a long time to get the power just right, between making sure that the ax stayed where I put it, as well as came to my hand when I reached for it."

"Awesome," Dennis told her.

And it was. He wished again briefly that he'd be able to master such a thing.

But his talents lay in other areas.

Or so he hoped.

<hr>

THE PATH UP THE HILL TO THE SACRED CAVE WAS obvious. Huge boulders rose up on either side, growing closer together as they neared the top, until they almost formed a solid wall. He could have slipped between two of them, but he doubted Christine in her full troll getup would have been able to.

Christine's air element kept blowing the stench of the place away from Dennis's face. Though now, underneath the stink of rotting fruit, came the smell of something more earthy. He figured it was a scent Christine would approve of.

The gravel under their feet gave way to more solid dirt. The opening of the cave loomed ominously in front of them. Christine could probably pass through with her ax in her hand, her arm stuck up all the way above her head, and still not touch the top.

Darkness and cold winds blew out from the opening. Dennis couldn't smell it, but he knew Christine could: magic filled the doorway.

Was that why Christine and Ty hadn't been able to find any dwelling places for the Longians? Because they actually lived on a different plane? Was it possible to set up a portal in midair? Christine had once explained that portals needed to be connected to the earth. Was that because she was a troll and was connected to the earth herself? Dennis would have to remember to ask her at some point.

Cautiously, Christine stepped close enough to the doorway to just stick her nose through.

She shook her head, sneezing as she backed away.

"It isn't a portal," she said, then she sneezed again. "Don't know what exactly it is."

"Any chance it opens up into midair when we step through?" Dennis asked. That was his main concern.

These were an air-born race. Would there actually be ground in their sacred space?

Christine shrugged. "Doesn't matter. I'll catch you if we start to fall," she promised him. Then she gave him a sly smile. "Probably."

Dennis snorted. This was the sister he remembered from recent years. The smartass, not the one who was so serious all the time.

She reached out and grabbed his hand. "Here goes nothing," she muttered.

"Naw, here goes us," Dennis said, giving her so much larger hand a squeeze.

She gave him another one of those smiles that had become so rare before they both stepped forward.

To Dennis, it felt more like stepping through a soap bubble than anything else. His ears popped, and he had to move his jaw around and swallow a couple more times to make them pop again.

A huge cave stood before him. It was made out of that same bleached white rock as the boulders outside. Glowing lights were set into the walls, so it was almost as bright as day. Plus, about four stories up, a roughly circular opening had been carved, showing the sky.

Crevices had been notched out of the walls, each about five feet across at the opening. They reminded Dennis of the ancient Catholic church he'd visited when he'd been in France and the stations of the cross that lined the main sanctuary. The hushed air certainly loaned the feeling of solemnity to the place.

He counted sixteen openings around the vaguely circular space. It made sense that the Longians would do counts of four, as they had four fingers as well as eight hands, though the bottom two acted more like feet.

The ground in here wasn't either dirt or gravel, but what looked like white clay, pounded down and smoothed instead of baked in a kiln or made into tiles.

No creatures rushed at them, no one challenged them. The space was empty.

Dennis found himself holding his breath. He released it slowly.

He understood at a gut level why this was considered a sacred space. It was wrapped in the feeling of holiness, like a shroud. Even though he doubted the Longians celebrated a god that he'd recognize, it was still obvious.

Gingerly, Dennis took a step forward. He carefully placed his feet when he realized that the floor had been sprinkled with the white substance and would show every one of his footsteps.

Christine followed, though she didn't seem as concerned about leaving footprints. Maybe it was because it was already too late, they'd already broken the sanctity of the place.

Dennis made his way to the first opening.

What the hell was that? It looked like a modern sculpture, carved out of white marble. About four feet tall and two feet wide, sitting atop a stone base. The sculpture had been polished so the marble was completely smooth and reflected the light in the room.

The bottom of the sculpture was rounded and solid. What looked like three trunks rose up from that, intertwined, with a couple of random holes punched through. It ended abruptly, cut off by something harsh, the top of it roughly hewn and unpolished.

Dennis turned to look at Christine. She looked as confused as he did.

Good to know he wasn't the only one who just didn't get modern art.

He walked over to the next piece. It didn't make any more sense to him. It looked like a triangle, carved out of that same white marble, though this slab had black streaks running through it. The center of the triangle had been hollowed out and four perfectly round balls dangled down.

"No idea," Dennis murmured as he moved on.

Each piece was like that, usually a geometric shape or weird carving. None of it made any sense to him. Most of the pieces had been carved out of the same white marble, though a couple appeared to come from a different region, as in addition to the black streaks were also veins of gold.

"So?" Christine asked after Dennis had walked around the room twice. "What do you think?"

"Haven't a clue," Dennis said. None of the pieces spoke to him or drew him in any way. Instead, they all struck him as alien. Nothing that would be a torso or body to him.

"Look again," Christine growled, sounding impatient.

With a nod, Dennis made his way back to the first piece, no longer caring so much about tracking footprints.

They'd already marred the floor. There was no hiding that they'd been here.

It kinda sorta looked like a torso to him. But a weird one. With limbs growing out of the center of it. But it didn't attract him. When he closed his eyes, nothing in the room drew his attention.

"We're in the wrong place," he finally admitted, turning to face Christine.

She was no longer looking at him.

Instead, her face was turned up toward the opening to the sky. "Incoming," she said. "Helmet!" she barked at him as she grabbed her ax.

Dennis gulped and put the helmet on, then backed away, stepping further into the small opening holding the carving of the torso-like-thingy.

Hopefully after Christine got their attention with her ax, the Longians would be willing to talk.

Otherwise, it was going to be one hell of a failed trip.

***

"We just want to talk!" Christine growled again as she smacked the snout of another Longian who came too near.

Dennis continued to hang back in the alcove of the first statue.

He didn't want to admit it, but his sister kinda frightened him when she went full on warrior princess troll mode.

Mind you, fighting a dozen flying centipedes had pissed her off.

Dennis had stayed out of the way as she'd requested, though he'd tried offering advice a couple of times, or at least told her when one of the Longians had tried to sneak up on her.

As awesomely muscled as his sister was, she was growing tired. He could tell.

And those damned long claws of the Longians weren't getting any duller.

Someone had to stop this madness.

The Longians weren't paying any attention to him. They kept their focus on the threat in the room, namely Christine.

Dennis contemplated knocking one of the statues over. That might get the Longians to stop, if he threatened to destroy all their hard work in their sacred space.

That just didn't seem right to Dennis, though. While showing strength was important to all the races of the *kith and kin* that he'd met, they also respected courage and bravery.

So that was what Dennis had to show them.

He gulped.

Or else face a messy death. He wasn't sure which at this point.

Slowly, Dennis removed his helmet. God, that thing really did weigh a ton. Sure, it would have protected him. But he had Christine to do that.

Next, he stripped off his armor, the ring mail. He dropped it beside the helmet.

He took another deep breath, still thankful for the air element of Christine's who allowed him to breathe. Then he stepped out from the alcove onto the main floor.

"Stop!" he commanded at the next beast who was about to take a swipe at Christine. "Stop!"

The beast shook its head in surprise as it banked and rose up in the air again.

A second one of the Longians aborted its run.

"Look, we just want to talk," Dennis said.

"Why should we talk with you, human?" asked one of the bigger Longians. It had a purple snout and white and black scales, and looked older than some of the others, some of the spikes on its tail sheared.

"We came to admire your great work," Dennis said, indicating the statues around him. "And to maybe commission a piece."

"Why didn't you say so in the first place?" the Longian demanded, flowing down to the ground and landing on his bottom limbs, balancing with his tail. His torso rose up at least fourteen feet from the ground.

"Because you were too busy attacking?" Christine growled.

"You're a troll. What do you know of art?" the Longian sneered.

"Don't answer that," Dennis warned his sister.

Christine snapped her jaw tight, not saying anything, though her glare spoke volumes.

"My name's Dennis," he said, nodding at the Longian.

"Du Ko," the Longian said in reply. "How did you hear of our sculptures? Though some of our artists are quite shy about advertising," he paused and glared at the bright yellow beast who landed bedside him, "I've been doing my best to get the word out."

"Oh, here and there," Dennis said. "You know, the Kalickium are quite jealous."

Though Dennis had no idea if the Kalickium had ever even heard of the Longians, it was a safe bet, as the Kalikium appeared to be jealous of just about everyone.

Du Ko preened. "Of course they are!" he said. "Their art forms really haven't developed much beyond primitive."

Dennis wasn't certain if Du Ko showing all his teeth counted as a big beaming smile, but Dennis had been around enough of the *kith and kin* to recognize a happy being.

"So what can you tell me about these pieces?" Dennis said, gesturing toward the first one.

"I would be delighted to give you a tour, although…" Du Ko paused as he looked around the rest of the room. "How about this?"

Dennis could recognize a deal about to be struck as well as anyone else.

"Why doesn't each artist come and explain their work to you? Then, when they're all finished, you can choose the artist you want to work with for your commissioned piece," Du Ko said.

"Only as long as I get to take selfies with each artist," Dennis said. "In front of their work."

"Of course!" Du Ko said. "That's an excellent idea!"

At least three-fourths of the races Dennis met with liked having their pictures taken. Particularly selfies, with him at the center. Most of the time the pictures disappeared off Dennis's phone as soon as he got home, but sometimes they'd reappear again once he went to one of the places that catered to the *kith and kin.*

He'd never be able to show off his grand collection of photographs. He was actually quite proud of many of them. They represented the hard work he'd done, bringing the *kith and kin* over to Christine's side, to fight in the war.

It didn't feel like work most of the time, schmoozing all the various beings, going out drinking with them, or even the one time he'd gone bowling with that group of orcs. (The human game lost something in translation, or so he'd been told, by using merely balls and not the polished skulls of your enemies.)

Still, Christine told Dennis regularly just how important his work was, how much it meant to her.

And now—time to listen to a bunch of artists brag about their work.

He supposed it would be better than sitting through yet another annual report meeting for his day job.

IT TURNED OUT THAT MOST ARTISTS DIDN'T HAVE A clue how to talk about their work, Human or Otherwise. Dennis had gone from wanting to gnaw his own arm off for a distraction to actively imagining killing the Longian standing beside him.

Christine was *so* going to owe Dennis big time after this.

Most of the artists had basically said, "It's a sculpture. It's pretty. I made it."

And that was it.

Others droned on and on about how the wind on the rock had inspired them, or how this curve reminded them of sleekness of their mate's wings, or even how the sculpture was supposed to capture that moment of surprise when an enemy turned on you.

This last artist, however, had decided to give a blow by blow description of every single influence that had struck him, how turning his sculpting knife from this side to that had created that last curve, how modern and sensible and yet expressive every line was.

At least Dennis had perfected the art of yawning with his mouth closed, all the while making appreciative and encouraging noises.

Finally, Du Ko came to Dennis's rescue. "That's very interesting, Kai Shan," he boomed. "I think that the human has a good enough idea of your style to be able to make a choice."

Actually, Dennis had made his choice long ago. The first piece had turned out to be Du Ko's work, and he'd actually been good at describing how it represented the three branches of wisdom—fighting, flying, and meditation—and how they got cut off before reaching fruition by death.

"You've made my decision very difficult," Dennis lied. He caught the eye of a couple of the artists, nodding in their direction. "However, I believe that the artist who is going to be most capable of capturing my vision is Du Ko."

The other Longians all clapped politely. Some only used their upper two hands, while a few actually seemed enthusiastic and clapped using two or three sets of hands.

Either that, or they were just suck-ups.

"Wonderful! Wonderful!" Du Ko said. He gave a sharp nod to the other Longians. One by one, they all departed, up through the center hole.

Then Du Ko turned to cast a dark eye on Christine. She'd been chatting with one of the other Longians, showing off her ax and comparing fighting techniques.

"The creation of art is always a private matter," Du Ko said slowly. "A holy bond not entered into lightly between the muse,"—here he indicated Dennis—"and the artist."

Dennis nodded. "I feel the same way. But this is my sister. And my patron, as it's her gold paying for your work." They hadn't started bargaining yet over price— Dennis figured they'd get to that once they figured out what the work entailed.

"Your sister, eh?" Du Ko said. He rubbed the underside of his chin with one hand. "You have an interesting history, particularly for a human," he concluded after a moment. "And a keen eye for the arts. And while I was of course flattered that you chose me for your artist, I have now decided to choose you, as well, for my muse."

"Ah, thanks," Dennis said. He had the feeling that he was entering into a much longer-term relationship than he'd bargained for.

But hey, maybe that meant that he'd be able to recruit the Longians for Christine's armies at some point.

"So what exactly did you have in mind?" Du Ko asked. He paced around Dennis, looking at all sides of him.

Dennis didn't really like feeling like a piece of beef. However, he knew this was where it was going to get tricky.

"Me," he said.

Du Ko nodded. "I'd already assumed that you were the model," he said dryly. "Anything in particular, though?"

Dennis glanced over at Christine, who shrugged.

"My torso," Dennis proclaimed.

"Show me," Du Ko said, waving his hand at Dennis, indicating that Dennis should take off his shirt.

Damn it. Dennis was just going to have to wear this shirt some other time, when it wasn't either going to be covered up with armor or crumpled on the floor.

Wait. That came out wrong.

Dennis lifted up his shirt and took it off. He had some muscles from playing racketball, though he'd let that slide recently. And he'd been drinking too much with the *kith and kin*, recruiting them for Christine's armies. He hadn't gotten out all summer, so all his skin was pasty white. Not that his skin allowed him to tan. He'd always envied Christine her ability to do that when they'd been kids. Not that he'd ever told her that.

The Longian nodded as he stared at Dennis, his black eyes intent on Dennis's skin.

Dennis fought the impulse to cross his arms over his chest and instead put his fists on his hips. He tried to flex his muscles, but that just made him hunch his back.

Sure, he was a pasty white guy. Not in the best of shape. And he really didn't like having to stand there and be looked at by one of the *kith and kin* who'd admitted that he found humans a pretty tasty dish, when cooked properly, of course.

"I'm assuming this is a private sculpture?" Du Ko asked after he'd walked around Dennis a few more times.

Dennis suddenly saw his opening. "It isn't, actually," he said. "This is part of an installation piece that is going to be given to the troops."

"Part of a larger body of work?" Du Ko asked. He sounded hopeful.

"Exactly," Dennis said. "Now, I can't guarantee the placement of your piece, particularly since I haven't seen it yet. However, if it comes out as spectacular as I'm assuming it will, it will be the centerpiece."

He wasn't about to try to explain how it would actually be part of the assembled obelisk of truth.

"When will it be unveiled?" Du Ko said.

Dennis could tell that the artist was already considering how to turn the opening into a marketing event.

"Sorry, it won't be a *public* public showing," Dennis explained. "It's just going to be for the troops of the *kith and kin* who have allied themselves with Christine. Princess Kizalynn Linumok Te'Dur. My sister."

"Oh. Oh!" Du Ko said, turning to suddenly stare at Christine.

Christine bristled in response, though Dennis could tell she was trying to keep it down. At least she wasn't growling. Yet.

Finally, Du Ko nodded. "I remember now. You were raised as a changeling, correct?"

Christine nodded.

"Hence, your brother," he said, indicating Dennis with his middle set of hands.

Christine nodded again.

"Princess, it will be my honor to sculpt the torso of your brother," Du Ko said.

"Thank you," Christine said.

Dennis could see the wheels turning inside Du Ko's head, wondering how he could turn this onetime gig into a permanent thing. He could already see Du Ko creating new business cards, ones that said *Royal Sculptor* on them.

Yup. This was definitely going to be a thing.

Now, they just had to settle the details.

DENNIS LET DU KO AND CHRISTINE BARGAIN WITH each other regarding price and materials. Dennis hadn't been raised to bargain—he was an American, so he generally accepted whatever price was listed on an item. Since a lot of the places he went to were run by the *kith and kin* and didn't have any prices listed at all, he'd had to learn. He'd also had to get good at it rather quickly, or he would have been spending half his paycheck every week on those he was supposedly recruiting.

Still, watching Christine in action was educational. She was apparently a natural when it came to driving a hard bargain. Probably her trollish nature coming to the forefront, along with her natural contrariness.

He was concerned at the first insult thrown between them, how Christine referred to Du Ko as an insect not fit for stepping on and Du Ko told Christine that he was surprised that, as a troll, Christine even understood that insects weren't just for eating.

Back and forth they went, until finally they reached an agreement.

Dennis would have to come back twice to sit for his piece. Du Ko would deliver the statue to the human plane in one week's time. Christine would deliver half the gold now, and the other half when the statue was complete.

Du Ko would create the portal for Dennis, though Christine had bargained hard for Du Ko to come to the human plane to do his work. However, the artist had insisted that his studio would produce the best results, and he would not be budged.

Finally, the bargaining was finished. Christine brought out a trunk of gold from one of the pocket spaces she'd fashioned for herself.

What, had she already had that planned? Was she used to carrying around trunks of gold? What else did she have stashed?

Then Dennis shook his head. He didn't want to know. That was the same dark rabbit hole as asking a woman what she carried in her purse.

Only when Dennis and Christine were finally back at her place on the human plane did Christine turn on Dennis. "Just what were you thinking? Taking off your armor? Showing your skin that way? You could have been killed!"

Dennis took a step back, surprised by the vehemence of her anger. "It seemed like a good idea at the time," he said. "They would have killed you."

"Or they would have killed you," Christine growled at him. "You didn't need to go to such an extreme."

"Yes, I did," Dennis said. "They wouldn't have respected anything less."

Christine growled low and deep in her throat. "They would have eventually respected my ax," she said.

Dennis sighed. "No, they wouldn't have. You could have killed all of them and then only more would have come. Death wasn't the way to get their attention."

Christine blew out her breath, obviously frustrated. "There must have been some other way. Not this stupidity. Just a single claw strike would have killed you."

"They weren't paying any attention to me," Dennis pointed out. "And you've told me before that winning the war isn't just about fighting."

Christine seemed to deflate at that. She transformed down, changing out of her full troll body into something that was an amalgamation of troll and human. Just a bit larger than Dennis, with more human girl curves but still a troll snout and tusks. "I didn't like it," she said, wanting to make her point.

"I understand that," Dennis said. "I can't, however, guarantee that I won't do it again."

"But why?" Christine asked, her rage boiling up again. "Why sacrifice yourself?"

Dennis shrugged. He'd never really considered it before. He just knew in his gut that he would.

Dennis wasn't really a contemplative kind of guy. He'd been accused of being as shallow as a mud puddle. Maybe the war had changed him as well. Maybe losing the *kith and kin* who he'd befriended had changed him.

The air in Christine's underground warren grew heavy with expectation. Dennis knew he had to answer his sister's question.

"If you lose, if the *kith and kin* end up allying themselves with the demons, all of humanity is lost, at least until the next turn of the wheel," Dennis said slowly. "My death will be worth it, if it will prevent that."

Christine paced away from him. Her posture was stretched tight, her hands at her side, clenching and unclenching.

"I wish I could order you away from the war," Christine said softly. "I wish I hadn't dragged you into it. You're supposed to be *safe*."

"But you wouldn't be this far along without me," Dennis pointed out. Or at least that was what she'd told him more than once.

Christine kept her back to him, but she nodded. "Without your efforts, the *kith and kin* would have already fallen."

He didn't know what that admission had cost her, but he knew that it hurt.

"Look, Sis, I don't plan on sacrificing myself. I have no death wish, believe me," Dennis said sincerely. He knew that there was an element of a lie at the very bottom of his words. On the bad nights, he might have considered ending it all. But the bad nights didn't come anywhere near as often now.

"But I also have a job to do," Dennis continued. "An important one. One that I'm good at, and that I actually like doing." He hadn't really thought about it before, but he realized that statement was more truthful than the previous one.

Christine finally looked at him over her shoulder, giving him a sly grin. "So once the war is over, should I hire you as head of my PR department?"

Dennis shrugged. "Or you could hire me now," he said.

Christine blinked, then nodded. "Done," she said.

Now it was Dennis's turn to take a step back, surprised. "You serious?" he asked.

Christine shrugged. "You've been working part time for me for a while, now. May as well make it official."

Dennis grinned at her. It actually felt like the right thing to do. Still, he had to say something. "That might make me more of a target," he warned.

Christine shrugged. "This is a hard truth, Dennis, that I'm willing to share with you and no one else. If we lose, yes, you'll be among those first killed. That is actually a good thing." Christine gave an expressive shudder. "Hell on earth will no longer merely be an expression. I would rather that you and the rest of my human family didn't have to live through that."

Dennis nodded. He knew that intellectually. However, the way Christine had just said it had driven the point home.

"In the meanwhile," Christine said, rounding on Dennis, "you have to promise me that you'll try harder not to be killed. Okay?"

"Sure," Dennis said easily. He really wasn't seeking his own death.

Particularly not now, when a whole new future appeared to be opening up before him.

***

Du Ko hadn't allowed Dennis to see the sculpture while it was still a work in progress.

However, the artist had finally declared it finished, and both Dennis and Christine had been invited to Du Ko's studio for the great unveiling.

The studio had turned out to be surprisingly comfortable. It existed in a pocket plane, on a world filled with huge trees that had long, knifelike leaves. Du Ko had built a small wooden platform strung between four of the trunks. The walls were all wood, polished to a golden, warm hue. Windows lined each side, giving Du Ko different light, at least according to him. (Dennis never saw sunlight—all light appeared to be filtered through various levels of leaves.) A long platform lay under one window, where Du Ko had Dennis stretch out on his side.

After Dennis had taken his shirt off, of course.

At least Dennis had felt less like a slab of beef and merely an object of interest once Du Ko had started working.

It had surprised Dennis that the Longians produced an acidic spit that would dissolve marble. Du Ko would spit into his hands, look at Dennis, then look back at the rock and use his hands to shape it. Sometimes he used a chisel, but mostly the artist molded the stone.

The work in progress had remained behind a large screen so that Dennis couldn't see it.

Finally, though, the unveiling was at hand.

"Welcome, welcome!" Du Ko said as Dennis and Christine stepped through the portal. At Dennis's suggestion, Christine had worn her human guise, appearing more like the sister he'd grown up with.

Du Ko handed them both a glass filled with what looked like a sparkling rosé, though Dennis knew from experience that it had more of a raspberry flavor, sweet and light.

"Thank you," Christine said as she took the glass. She looked around, obviously uncomfortable. "Nice place," she still said. Trolls were all about good earth and living underground. Being this high up in the trees, surrounded by wood, wasn't her thing at all.

Du Ko beamed at her. "Thank you, princess," he said. "It's the first test of a true artist to be able to create their own space."

Dennis nodded as he accepted his own glass. He'd heard the story before. He wasn't about to tell Du Ko that these sorts of spaces came naturally to humans. While the Longian had turned out to be okay, he still had a lot of prejudice when it came to humans, as well as a true hatred for trolls. No matter what Dennis said about the virtues of his sister, Du Ko had an anecdote or a story that countered it.

While getting the artist to create the statue had been a success, even the promise of a general unveiling in a public ceremony hadn't been enough enticement to get Du Ko to join the side of the *kith and kin*.

However, at least Dennis had the feeling that the

Longians would remain neutral and not go fight on the side of the demons.

"First off, I'd like to thank my patron, Princess Kizalynn Linumok Te'Dur," Du Ko announced, holding his glass up in a toast, as if practicing the speech he'd give at a public unveiling.

Christine nodded and played the part, giving the Longian a huge smile.

Huh. She almost looked sincere.

"Next, I need to thank my muse, Dennis," Du Ko said, raising his glass to Dennis. "Nothing is possible without inspiration," he continued.

"And finally, I thank my family, as well as the Creator, for giving me the opportunity to continue to express my truest self. Blessed be!" he called out, raising his glass to the air for the final toast.

"Blessed be," Dennis intoned in response. He nudged Christine to get her to do the same.

Really, had she not learned anything from dealing with the other *kith and kin*?

"Without further ado, I'd like to show you my latest masterpiece," Du Ko said. He walked to the side of the statue that dominated the center of the studio, discretely covered by a huge cloth. "I call it, The Torso."

With three hands, the Longian pulled away the cloth.

"Ohhh," Dennis said, as he'd prepared himself to.

It was, of course, different than what he'd expected.

It looked nothing like a torso. Du Ko, like the rest of the Longians, wasn't into representational art. That was beneath them. Only weirdos or painters did that.

The piece looked very similar to the first piece of

artwork that Dennis had seen by the Longian. The base was round, solid, and well-polished. Growing up from there were four round limbs, intertwining. However, instead of all of them reaching up, only three did. One flowed out from roughly the center of the piece, reaching down, tapering off before it reached the end of the base. The other three appeared to be stretching up, reaching for different prizes.

Dennis had no idea what the heck it meant.

"Could the artist give some more commentary on his work? So that I can explain it better when I show it," Christine said.

Dennis nodded his approval. That was a really nice touch.

"Of course!" Du Ko beamed at the pair of them. "The four branches represent the four aspects of my muse, of course," he said. "The first is the root, the family, from which everything else flows."

Dennis could see that now that Du Ko had mentioned it. But what were the other three aspects?

"Then, we have the striving for immortality that all humans inherently reach for," Du Ko said, a touch of chiding in his voice.

Immortality? Really? Him? Huh. Dennis hadn't thought he did that. But maybe that was just Du Ko's generally opinion of humans.

"There's the fighting aspect, of course," Du Ko said, pointing toward one limb that appeared to be reaching back, behind the statue. "Then there's the mating part."

When Dennis looked closely, he could see that the end of the limb was split into many smaller branches, merely hinted at with indentations, not actually separated.

"Then there is the greatest part of all—man's attempt to reach for the arts, to become one with the Creator," Du Ko said, indicating the limb that reached straight upward.

"Very interesting," Christine said, taking a step forward. "May I?" she asked, indicating that she wanted to walk all the way around the statue.

"Be my guest," Du Ko beamed.

Dennis stayed where he was, studying the front of the piece.

Was that him? Was that his piece? Was that the piece that Christine needed in order to assemble the obelisk of truth?

He closed his eyes for a moment, trying to feel if the piece tugged at him, gave him some indication of rightness.

He felt nothing.

Dennis didn't want to admit it; however, he was very much afraid that he was going to be letting his sister down. This wasn't the piece, wasn't *his* piece.

"Why don't you take a closer look?" Du Ko suggested in a quiet voice.

Dennis merely nodded and walked forward. How could he explain to the Longian what he was feeling? That he didn't see any part of himself in this sculpture?

It wasn't until Dennis got very close, almost on top of it, that he finally saw the words. They were very faint, scratched with a thin line across the top of the torso.

Born ready.

That was it. That was what had been missing.

Suddenly, Dennis felt in tune with the rock. It was an odd sensation, as if his own torso had momentarily been replaced with the statue, those four limbs reaching out for immortality, infinity, future and past all at the same time.

He took a deep gulp of air and stepped back, overwhelmed. He blinked rapidly. Damn it! He wasn't about to cry. Not now. Not here.

"Thank you," Dennis said, looking up at the Longian.

Christine shot him a worried look.

Dennis used his palms to squish out the tears that had suddenly formed. He understood, now, everything that the Longian had been trying to say, how Dennis was searching for some sort of immortality, something bigger than himself.

Was this why humans had such a fervent belief in God? That was never going to be Dennis's way. Instead, he was going to force his way into something bigger than himself. Like a family. Like the war.

"You see," Du Ko said, his voice reverent. "I didn't know if you would, if a human could truly appreciate the higher art of the Longians."

Dennis didn't roll his eyes, though it was a close thing. Of course, the Longians considered themselves the highest on the food chain. Most of the *kith and kin* did to some extent, though the Longians took it to an extreme.

Du Ko heaved a deep sigh. "I have a confession to make," he said slowly. "I've failed at my conversations with the others, to get the Longians as a race to commit to your war," he said, nodding at Christine.

"Thank you for trying," Dennis said. And he meant it.

He hadn't thought that Du Ko had been listening to any of his stories.

"I have gotten a small continent of fighters, however, to join the cause," Du Ko said. He nodded his head at Christine. "Given your approval, of course."

"I will happily take any warriors you can muster," she said sincerely. She gave him a wide grin. "Though I cannot guarantee their survival."

Dennis nodded. That was generally the right tactic to take with the *kith and kin*. Tell them that they were about to die in glorious battle. It was what some of the races appeared to live for.

"Then I am glad that I finished this one final masterpiece," Du Ko said.

"As am I," Dennis chimed in.

"Maybe after the war, you will sit for me again," Du Ko said. "I have some ideas…"

"Gladly," Dennis said. "After the war."

He didn't know if there would be an after the war for him. For his family. For anyone he knew.

Still, he vowed to keep a hopeful attitude.

After all, he had been born ready for all of this.

CHAPTER EIGHTEEN

Nik knew better.

Really. He did.

He just couldn't seem to help himself, though. It wasn't that he was being influenced by demons, or even by humans. It just…it seemed like the right thing to do, though he knew it wasn't.

But when the Risilodan, or the rowdy boys as Christine called them, came in for supplies, he found himself making some suggestions even before they asked for his help.

And possibly, maybe, he suggested the ingredients that an enterprising young magic worker could use to counter the spell that he'd just sold to the demons who'd just left.

Nik couldn't believe the words coming out of his mouth. He did *not* do that sort of thing. He was neutral. He sold to all parties. He did not give advice like this to the demons. Why was he giving it to the rowdy boys? Without being asked?

As soon as the rowdy boys left, Nik flipped the portals

closed. He didn't want any more visitors, not until he figured this out.

He walked back into the backroom, letting the heavy curtain cut him off from the rest of the world. The workbench was clear, though boxes still lined the shelves on the walls. Nik had thought about just putting all those boxes back into the warehouse, as they continued to remind him that Christine hadn't come by to work for him in ages.

Then again, there was the possibility that the empty shelves would be worse.

He pulled together the ingredients to run spells meant to detect influence, demonic or otherwise. Good French lavender, aged red cedar bark, sand from what was now known as Saudi Arabia, dried black-widow spider webs, dust from a forgotten tomb, crumbled charcoal.

At the completion of the first spell, tiny tracks showed up in the crumbled charcoal, as if it had been brushed with a feather.

Huh. Heavenly influence? But a really light touch, if it existed at all.

However, every spell he ran after that, the charcoal remained completely flat, which meant that there was no influence, demonic or heavenly, skewing Nik's actions.

The first indication must have been a fluke, a false positive.

Those happened. It was why Nik always included double the amount of ingredients for certain spells, encouraging the magicians to run those spells more than once.

Influence detection spells were notoriously finicky, as

well as not practical and occasionally unreliable. Ages ago, Nik had believed the outcome of the simple spells he'd cast, when he'd been human, not realizing that he'd already been corrupted, the demons influencing his thoughts and actions. He had perfected the spells he currently used over the centuries, and felt fairly confident in their reliability.

Still, that first false positive worried him. Particularly when he heard the whooshing sound that only a pair of heavy, powerful wings could make.

With a sigh, Nik put aside his spell ingredients and walked back out into the main room.

The angel dominated the room, despite the tall ceilings and multiple rows of shelves. Nik automatically squinted up at the lights, trying to determine what setting they were on.

It never hurt to check what level of light an angel might prefer for shopping. That sort of knowledge might come in handy someday.

But the angel cast too much of her own damned glow for him to be able to tell.

She wore gray robes that afternoon that flowed down to the ground, with no sleeves. That indicated this was more of a social call. The official uniform called for the brightest white robes and completely covered up.

Her hair was still the same bright shining gold that Nik remembered from all those years ago. Her eyes were gray, like morning storm clouds. They always seemed familiar, even the first time he'd met her. She had dark skin, almost incongruous with her blonde hair, except she made it work. Her features were petite, her nose small, her lips thin, her perfect, shell-like ears just peeking out from under her bob.

"Svetlana," Nik said. He forced himself to smile, though he had no idea if the spell that animated his painted on features worked with angels.

As she gave him a quick smile back, he had to assume that it was. At least for now.

"Nikolai," she said, her smile growing sad. "Why did you recommend the disarming crystals and the red oak potions to your most recent clients?"

"Honestly Svetlana? I don't know," he said. "I was just running influence spells in the back, to see if I could figure out why. But I don't believe I'm under any sort of influence." Nik hadn't meant to tell her that. Just her presence seemed to always loosen his tongue.

"You know that helping one client to the detriment of others endangers your neutrality," Svetlana warned. "You must be more careful. Particularly since you turned in that demon book of accounting."

Nik nodded. It had been over five years since he'd given that book to the Host. Still, he'd known at the time that it had looked bad.

"You know that it wasn't because I wasn't neutral that I turned that in, right? I turned it in because it proved that members of the Host had been compromised," Nik pointed out.

"Which is why no one came to warn you when you did it," Svetlana replied. "However. The advice you just gave was not neutral. You were using information you'd just gained from your demon clients to aid your non-demon clients, ones in direct conflict."

Nik hung his head. He knew better. He did! "I don't know what happened," Nik said softly.

He knew that the angel wouldn't touch him. Still, her soft voice felt as warm and as light as a caress. "You must see that it doesn't happen again."

Nik's head came up. "Or else?" he asked. He knew what she might say. He needed to hear her actually say it.

"Or else you will have broken our agreement," Svetlana said. Her voice changed from comforting to whip-cracking hard. "I will be forced to end our bargain. You will no longer be able to inhabit this wooden being."

"I will die," Nik said flatly.

The angel gave him a sad smile. "In a way, yes. But—"

"I know, I know," Nik interrupted. Heavenly ever after wasn't what he considered an ideal existence. He paused, then added, "Christine is on a quest, sent by the oracles."

Svetlana nodded. "And you are to have no part of it."

"But—"

"None," Svetlana said, her voice thundering like doom across the shop. "If you value your precious immortality, such as it is, you cannot help her. That would be in direct conflict with your neutrality."

Nik sighed. "Understood."

The angel sighed as well. "I wish it wasn't that way," she said. "But if wishes were horses…"

"Everyone would ride," Nik replied. It was an old saying, something his grandmother had possibly told him.

"Exactly." Svetlana paused. "It was good to see you again, Nikolai."

Nik wasn't sure why she had such a wistful tone in her

voice. Or maybe he was just imagining it. "It was a pleasure," he assured her.

Though that wasn't exactly true. After the angel disappeared (again, with that great swooping sound, as if she actually flew out of his shop instead of just vanishing) Nick always felt a great disquiet. As if he were a disappointment to the angel.

No matter. She was just another angel.

Nik walked back into his backroom and cleaned up all the ingredients there.

He didn't know what he was going to do when Christine came and asked him for the mirror of truth. He'd been hoping that if he bargained hard enough, he'd be able to just sell it to her.

Could he hand it to someone else? Have them sell it to her?

Why did Svetlana consider Nik giving the mirror to Christine to be going against his neutrality? Was it because Christine didn't have to fight or give up anything in order to get it?

Or was it because Nik would gladly give it to her, because it meant that she'd finally have a fighting chance? That it would mean the difference between the demons winning the war, or Christine and the *kith and kin*?

Try as he might, Nik couldn't remember when he'd acquired that mirror. He felt as if he'd always had it. Had Svetlana given it to him? Maybe.

He pulled the mirror out of its pocket space again. This time, he removed the lace doily from the front of it.

A human face stared back at him. Nik vaguely recognized it. The face had once been his. His wooden face resembled it, with the same dark eyebrows and wide-set eyes. But the man who stared out at him had more expression than Nik could ever manage with his spells, with soulful eyes and crinkles around his mouth that showed this man smiled often.

With a sigh, Nik covered the mirror back up and placed it into the pocket space again. The mirror showed the truth of whatever it was reflecting. Nik didn't understand why it showed his human face and not his wooden one, but he'd come to understand it showed the spirit of the thing, not the covering.

Nik straightened up and flipped the portals for the store to open again.

He was damned if he was going to break his word to Svetlana. He would remain strictly neutral in all his dealings from now on.

That was, until he saw Christine again.

CHAPTER NINETEEN

Buddy couldn't help but chortle when the latest three-inch thick report from Lars about the state of the war landed in the center of Buddy's sturdy, granite desk. He'd been relaxing in his office that morning, feet up on the desk, contemplating wandering down to the kitchen and snagging himself another long pork taco. Or maybe a nap. Possibly both.

Of course, he didn't torture himself by trying to read the damned thing. No, he had minions for that. Lesser demons who would read every line and sum all the real news down to bullet points. Generally, he assigned big important lawyers who considered themselves above such things until they learned better.

What Lars didn't realize was that by trying to obfuscate the facts of the war, it showed a huge tell, like a bullseye in the center of his long, sleek forehead. Lars wasn't much of a poker player. Chess, maybe, but not poker.

It wasn't that the demons were losing. Oh, no, Buddy

had separate means of verifying that they were, in fact, winning.

Lars was trying to hide just how imminent that win was.

Which in turn meant that he'd finally figured out just how vulnerable he'd be once the war was over.

Buddy had to hand it to the boy. He was a smart one. Too smart for his own good. Too well planned and organized.

While winning seemed inevitable, Buddy knew better than to count on it. He kept his options open instead, with a plan for Lars' soul should they lose, one that wouldn't let the boy squirrel in so much on himself and *plan* as he had.

Buddy would *not* sabotage the war effort. He'd actually stopped one of the other princes from doing so. (Though in Zaatar's defense, it wasn't because he'd thought the consequences through. He was just pissed that it wasn't him leading the last, final charge.)

No, Buddy had to make sure that his hands were clean no matter what happened, if they won or they lost.

Instead, Buddy focused on the other players around the table, as a good poker player did.

And there was one now.

"Come on in!" he replied to the knock he heard at the door.

The demon who slinked in was tall and slender for her kind, with spiked wings, nasty looking fangs, and glowing golden eyes. Her scales ranged in color from polluted white on her face to icy blue across her belly and back. She resembled Lars in superficial ways, like her long snout, her tail armed with spikes, and her graceful clawed hands.

All of which, Buddy knew, would make her attractive to Lars.

Except that Curly, as Lars had aptly named the bald demon, had always been in Buddy's pocket. She'd adopted a voice certain to ensure that Lars wouldn't necessarily listen to Curly, and instead, would discount anything she said.

When a new idea occurred to Lars, it wasn't because Curly had planted those words in his head. No, it was a thought that was brand new to him, not because he'd heard it before.

Curly's influence had worked brilliantly so far. And Lars had no idea whatsoever that she was a spy.

"What do you have to report?" Buddy asked, taking his feet down from the top of his desk.

"We are in the process of turning the *kith and kin* against each other," Curly told him, her voice smooth and silky, a warm alto that even made Buddy consider things other than the war.

However, Buddy knew this news from the other reports. "And?" he asked.

"We're within a few days of the final charge," Curly replied. "Lars intends on challenging Christine to battle, then slaying her. Once she falls, the rest of the *kith and kin* will ally themselves with their proper masters, the demons." Curly sniffed with disapproval. She'd never hidden her dislike or distrust of the *kith and kin*, considering them, as well as the humans, as far beneath her.

Buddy wasn't about to try to educate her on how it was better to use your allies and not just slaughter them when they didn't live up to their end of the bargain. It was too good of a lever he could use to control her.

"How will he get her to accept?" Buddy asked. "Just challenging her won't be enough."

"He has a threat worked up," Curly said. "Not her family, because that will piss her off too much, make her feel cornered and fight too hard. But one of the races of the *kith and kin* that she holds dear."

Curly couldn't help but roll her eyes at the sentiment. Another weakness of hers, that she held nothing dear, as it were. She felt that freed her from sentiment and didn't allow others to control her.

It was yet another blind spot that Buddy used ruthlessly to his advantage.

"So he threatens this entire race, she goes there to defend them, and he just shows up to fight her?" Buddy asked. There had to be something else to the plan. That seemed far too straightforward for Lars.

Curly shrugged. "This is where it gets difficult, boss," she admitted. "Lars actually has several contingency plans. If just threatening the race makes her show up, that's what he'll do. If he has to start the fight slowly, so that some can get away to tell her about their dilemma, he'll do that. If he has to stop the battle and call her into individual combat, he'll do that." Curly shook her head. "Lars has a whole fucking contingency map worked out, with branches spreading across it like some goddamned hippy forest." She shuddered.

"And you are ready for when Christine falls?" Buddy asked.

"Affirmative, boss," Curly said. "After the celebrations, and those will run for days, if not weeks, I'll show up at Lars' place with my new voice in place." She gave him an evil grin. "You think he'll fall for this one, don't you?" Her tone lowered and the way she flicked her black tongue around one of her lower fangs made Buddy shiver. She sounded like sex itself, slightly breathless and ready for round two. Or maybe three, but who was counting.

"Yup. That would do it," Buddy said, his own erection making him slightly uncomfortable. "And he won't suspect anything?"

Curly laughed, still in that deep-throated tone that sent shivers down Buddy's spine. She must have been practicing with the succubae, or possibly she was part succubus, he wasn't quite sure.

"He won't see the knife coming," Curly assured Buddy.

And really, that was all Buddy could ask for.

CHAPTER TWENTY

Tina found her heart kept racing while she went through her morning routing, waiting for Christine to show up.

Finally, Tina was ready.

Her adoptive parents, Mr. and Mrs. Zimmerman (because really, those people weren't her bio-parents, and while they'd helped her recover, they didn't mean that much to her anymore) had both had the sense to leave her alone, after inquiring about her previous night's sleep, as well as her preference for toast or English muffin.

Tina had felt her magic return to her slowly, day by day. There were still bad days when it felt as though her magic was blocked, when she felt her head full of cotton batting and unable to form a simple spell.

There were more good days than bad, though. Like that morning. When power sparked in her blood, making everything the sunshine touched seem to sparkle. When magic came as naturally to her as breathing. When it took no effort at all to tap the side of her mug of coffee and have the perfect amount of cream and honey magically added to it.

At least her adoptive parents didn't say anything at the display. Tina had gotten tired of the screaming matches when they tried to warn her about not wearing herself out or for ostentatious shows of magic.

They didn't get it. They didn't understand how Tina needed to prove to herself just how easy magic was on a good day. She wouldn't get tired. She had found new depths to draw on. Depths they had no idea about.

She felt sorry for her adoptive parents, in a way. They were both powerful magicians. They'd done their best to train her. However, they didn't have a clue what actual power was.

Somedays, Tina made the effort to be their bubbly little girl again. It was a safe place for her, a protected place. They seemed to appreciate it, breathing easier and not exchanging so many worried looks with one another.

This morning, Tina sparked with energy, ready to take on the world. And her adoptive parents knew enough to stay the hell out of her way.

Finally, Tina felt strong enough to take on Christine herself.

Not that Tina ever gave the slightest hint of that. No, she played the good girl to the hilt whenever Christine's name was mentioned, even going so far as to pretend that she missed the stupid troll.

Tina had managed to fool them all into trusting her again.

A polite knock on the front door had Tina practically levitating out of her seat. "I'll get it!" she called out so that Maria, the maid, couldn't get to the front door first.

"Hi!" Tina said as she flung open the door. She threw all her girlish enthusiasm into that single word, as if she were truly her old self once more.

Christine stood on the other side of the door in her full human guise. She was good at that, now. It took a lot of effort for Tina to see the troll underneath.

However, she always knew the beast was there.

Today, Christine wore a long-sleeved white shirt, something tight that showed off her curves, so different from Tina's skinny self. Tina had to admit that her short pixie cut looked cute, and that perhaps the perm had been a bad idea. Hell, Christine even had some makeup on, a brownish-red lipstick that highlighted her skin perfectly. She wore brown capris and stupid looking "barefoot" shoes that separated out her toes.

Tina was in blacks today. Black sleeveless vest/shirt that showed off her clear, white skin, a black jeans-skirt that made her outfit dressy, but not too much, along with rugged black sandals.

Christine paused at the edge of the threshold. "Hi," she said, cautiously, looking carefully at Tina. "You ready to go today?"

Tina hrumphed at that. "Of course I am!" she said. Her tone wasn't that whiny.

Though okay, maybe Christine had a point. Tina did have bad days still.

"Today's a good day," Tina assured Christine.

"Good," Christine said, giving her a smile. "I really need your help."

Tina would have killed to hear those words even as much as two weeks ago.

Now, well, she might kill anyway.

———

Christine had explained to Tina how they had to go find this thing that was supposed to be "Tina's Head." They were going to the plane of the Sammuthians. It was yet another branch of the *kith and kin*; however, they were more closely related to demons than most. They weren't the cambions, who were technically half demon. But they weren't that far away, either, in terms of the family tree.

Tina would just bet that was all Christine wanted, this other "item."

Christine had already stolen Tina's Destiny. Evidently, that wasn't enough, and now Christine wanted Tina's head as well.

She wouldn't get it. Tina was prepared to fight.

Christine had warned Tina that the Sammuthains were unusual before they went through the portal.

That wasn't the half of it, or so Tina realized as soon as they stepped into the bright, sunny world.

The sky was a pale gray, as though covered with high clouds. The sun looked like a bright white ball in the sky. Searingly bright green trees rose up just beyond the clearing they stood in, looking more like soft yew trees than prickly pines. The grass at their feet had turned golden in the bright sunlight, the ground baked a light brown color and smelling like the end of summer.

Streams of birds flew at them, coming from all sides.

No, those weren't birds.

Those were eyes.

Horrible, bloodshot eyes. The biggest had to be the size of Tina's palm, easy enough to slap away, while the smaller ones weren't any bigger than her pinky finger, and probably as annoying as gnats.

The irises were just as bad, coming in unnatural colors, like red, orange, purple, and even sickly yellow-gold.

The eyes flew around Tina and Christine in a tight circle, holding them in place.

Tina found her palm itching to grab her wand.

"Hold," Christine said softly.

She'd transformed into her troll self, though not fully, with more curves than a normal troll, taller than Tina, but not full troll height.

What, was that supposed to put Tina more at ease? No, Tina would rather see the full face of her enemy.

Still, Tina didn't grab for her wand. She kept a defensive spell locked in her mind, though, the first spell to go up when these nasty creatures attacked.

"They won't attack us unless we attack first," Christine said quietly, reminding Tina. "We just have to wait until the king arrives."

Tina couldn't help but snort. King? King of the Eyeballs? Great. Another one of the *kith and kin* who'd gotten too big for themselves.

Humans had proper royalty. Monarchies that had gone back thousands of years. Not these dumbos.

"Okay," Tina said after Christine threw her a look.

"Just trying to imagine what the king of the Sammuthians looks like."

"I know, right?" Christine said with a grin. "Does he have a little gold cape trailing behind him?"

Tina snorted again. For a moment, her hard mask faltered. She suddenly remembered how much fun she'd once had with Christine exploring the wild side of Seattle. Even the more quiet times, in their favorite coffee shop, talking about authors and books.

But that had been Before. Before Tina had realized the true cause of her current predicament. The real reason why her Destiny was muddled.

Off in the distance, a huge eyeball floated toward them. It appeared to have an entire retinue of smaller eyeballs rolling along behind it. Not quite a gold cape, but it definitely gave the impression of one.

The King had arrived. He had what Tina would have called a royal purple iris, and the white part wasn't quite as bloodshot as the other eyeballs. He was probably an inch or so bigger all the way around than all of the other eyeballs. He'd overfill Tina's palm with his mass, like a kid's squishy football.

"Greetings, O Travelers!" the king called out to them, placing great emphasis on each word.

Tina wasn't sure exactly how the eyeball spoke. It didn't have tiny vocal chords hidden away behind the eye, did it? No, that looked perfectly smooth. But the voice sounded as though the words were spoken out loud, not carried to them with magic.

Christine seemed surprised to be addressed as such.

"Do I have the pleasure of addressing the King of the Sammuthians?"

"King Sam Himself, At Your Service!" the eyeball replied.

Why were the words all coming out so strangely emphasized? Was that because of the spell that enabled him to talk?

"King Sam," Christine said, bowing her head slightly. "I am Princess Kizalynn Linumok Te'Dur. This is my human sister, Tina Zimmerman."

Of course, only Christine had such a fancy title. Just wait until Tina got her Destiny back. Then she'd be the one with the title, like "Savior of the World" or maybe "Protector of the Just."

But Tina didn't say anything negative out loud, and she hadn't for weeks. Instead, she gave her best smile to the eyeball (ugh) and bowed her head.

"What Wonders Do You Seek?" King Sam asked.

"What wonders would your majesty have to show us?" Christine asked. She seemed surprised.

Tina was curious as well. What sort of "wonders" did these eyeballs have?

King Sam appeared to think for a moment. "There is the Grotto of Many Mirrors," he said, "which has received five star reviews from most visitors." His voice finally changed to something more conversational, instead of having to Announce and Enunciate every word. "Also, the Waterfalls of Hidden Views, which *Travelers Today* proclaimed a true marvel worthy of every visitor. Plus the Head of Soul's Hill, with magnificent vistas, always a crowd pleaser, and one of my personal favorites." The king paused. If he'd had a throat, Tina would have sworn he cleared it. "Choose Your Adventure!" he announced, his voice booming.

A whispering hiss surrounded them. It took Tina a moment to realize it was all the other eyeballs urging them to go to one site or another.

It felt like a bad game show.

"We choose the Head of Soul's Hill," Christine said, as if there had been any doubt.

The crowd went wild, the eyeballs zooming up and down and around, all cheering madly.

King Sam waited until the ruckus had died down before he Announced, "Well Chosen. Sure to be The Adventure of a Lifetime!"

Really, why couldn't this eyeball just speak plainly?

Tina could tell that Christine's smile was just plastered on. She knew that Christine was having a hard time not rolling her own eyes at King Sam's proclamations.

If only Tina and Christine weren't mortal enemies. They'd probably be having fun at this point.

Tina forced herself to remember how bad the last few months had been, losing her magic. How powerless she'd felt.

While being friends with Christine was nice, it didn't compare to regaining her power. Her Destiny.

It was just a matter of time before Tina would get her revenge and take everything back.

It appeared that King Sam would act as their

guide to the Head of Soul's Hill. He gave a running commentary on everything they passed, telling them about the extremely bright trees and how the berries were used to make a beautiful blue-colored liqueur (and that they should be sure to pick some up in the Grand Market that they'd stop in at the end of their tour). The cheery river they walked beside had its start in the Endless Peaks to the east, the tips covered in snow, a sight not to be missed.

Finally, Tina was able to get in a word edgewise. "Do you give this sort of tour to every guest?" she asked. Wouldn't a king have other things to do and not just escort tourists around?

If an eyeball could have any sort of expression, just by itself, Tina would say that King Sam looked thoughtful. Then the eyeball bobbed up and down once, like a person nodding their head.

"We take turns being King," he admitted. "Today is merely my day. If you leave me a good review, I'll go into the short cycle, and my turn will come around again quickly, instead of staying in the long cycle that I'm on now."

"Okay," Christine said, sounding perplexed. "Where would we go to leave a review?"

Again, it was difficult, if not impossible, to read the expression of a mere eyeball. But if Tina could hazard a guess, she would say that King Sam beamed at them in joy.

"All the details will be on your Survey Exit Cards," he said proudly. "That way, you don't have to guess!"

"Very clever," Christine said.

That made King Sam beam more. "Thank you," he said with a little bob again. "I helped with the design."

Tina couldn't even imagine how an eyeball made a printed survey card. But then again, with magic, most anything was possible.

They quickly arrived at the foot of a steep hill. The top appeared to be covered with fog.

"Is it a good day to climb to the top?" Christine asked. "Will we be able to see anything?"

"The fog merely obscures the path on the way up, giving a Mythical Experience during your climb. It will Melt as you approach the top," King Sam reassured them, "giving you Majestic Views both Inside and Out."

Tina looked at the steep, winding path. While a troll could climb all day, and Christine was certainly muscled enough that she wouldn't get winded, Tina didn't have the strength she'd once had.

Plus, she didn't want to use up all her energy climbing. She needed to save some for the fight with Christine. Once they got to the top, Tina could challenge her. Maybe throw her down from the highest point.

"Do we really have to climb that?" Tina asked. She didn't mean to sound whiny but she couldn't help it. It looked like such a chore.

Christine threw her a worried glance. "My friend has been sick recently," she said quietly.

"You had merely to let us know!" King Sam said. He gave a whistling call.

Several of the smaller eyeballs darted forward. What had looked like a large boulder at the side of the path suddenly transformed into a set of stairs. They were carved out of rock, and instead of snaking up the side of the hill, went straight up. Climbing the stairs would still take effort. It would be much easier to just float up them, as well as a lot quicker.

"There are other sites that are ADA compliant," King Sam assured them. "The shortcut is the best that we've done so far with the Head of Soul's Hill. We would like to put in an elevator; however, that ruins the effect of passing through the mists and achieving the peak. Once we figure out how to recreate that effect for all our visitors and can settle on a design, we will put one in place." He paused, then glanced from Christine to Tina and back again. "Will this suffice?"

Christine looked at Tina, who nodded. "It's perfect," she announced.

Before King Sam could turn and proceed them up the stairs, Tina asked, "Can we continue on our own?"

Though the eyeball didn't have any eyelids, Tina still had the impression that it blinked at her. Several times.

"I just feel that's the right thing for us to do," Tina said quietly. "The right method for us to continue our quest."

"Ah! A Quest! A Quest!" the king said, loud enough for all of the eyeballs following them to be able to hear.

Tina didn't have to turn to look to see the mad celebrations that had broken out, the eyeballs whizzing around madly.

"Certainly! Please, Be Our Guests!" King Sam said, bobbing again, then flying to the side so Christine and Tina could proceed to walk to the stairs by themselves.

"You'll be sure to mention that in your Survey Exit

Cards, won't you?" King Sam enquired quietly, flying next to them. "In the Comments Section."

"Sure," Tina said breezily. She knew that the Sammuthians would take their comments and put them on their brochures, proclaiming this site as part of the quest for the Obelisk of Truth.

Maybe when Tina filled out the Survey Exit Card, she could also explain her quest to regain her Destiny.

It would probably bring in a lot more tourists than merely Christine's simple quest.

———

TINA EASILY FLOWED UP THE STAIRS, HER MAGIC lifting her up and carrying her along. It made her want to laugh. Christine marched solidly behind her, too stubborn to use her own magic.

Who would want to walk when you could fly?

Christine said that the workout would be good for her. Build up her stamina.

Ugh. Stupid troll.

The air smelled like a pine forest up here. Cool breezes wafted around them, keeping them from overheating. The rock steps had florets, trailing ivy, and even waves carved into the face of them. Flowing off on either side of the stairs was a dense forest, with thick brambles growing up between the rough tree trunks. Bees hummed every now and again, and a few birds bravely sang out.

Tina did have to admit that it was charming how the fog wreathed the forest surrounding them, wrapping around the trees, melting as they approached.

Every once in a while the stairs would turn and suddenly they'd have a marvelous view of the entire land surrounding them. She wouldn't have guessed that there would be so much agriculture in the area. The fields were postage stamp picture perfect.

Then again, that was probably the point. The Sammuthians might not have actually been growing much of anything. It could all be for show.

Off in the distance, Tina saw a glimmer of water. The beaches here were probably awesome. She might have to come back someday to see some of the other sights.

After she had regained her Destiny and won the Great War.

Tina slowed as she approached a thicker area of fog that actually covered the stairs.

Christine came up beside her, then looked up at her. "We should walk the rest of the way together," she said.

Tina pouted but acquiesced. "Fine," she said. She floated down to the ground. The rock felt cold under her feet.

Besides, maybe it was better for them to be next to each other. Easier for Tina to attack Christine that way.

The stairs grew more shallow as well as more primitive, as if the constant rain and moisture up here had worn grooves into the rock. The bramble between the trees grew less dense, and the trees themselves were shorter. Colder winds blew around them, carrying the smell of wet rock.

Side by side, they climbed the broad stairs. As promised, the mist melted away in front of them and the area before them opened up.

Tina caught her breath.

Okay, so maybe the view from up here really was spectacular.

She hadn't been expecting there to be a secondary set of hills just below them, with a wide lake scooped out. The waters brilliantly reflected the white sky, taking on a silvery appearance. Bleached rocks surrounded the lake, a stark contrast to the bright green trees growing just beyond. A sole hawk gave a loud cry, echoing off the peaks.

Tina turned slowly, marveling at the other vistas. The patchwork of fields stretched out in one direction, while forests marched on in another. It was easier to see the long stretch of ocean in the distance.

"Look there!" Christine proclaimed, sounding excited.

"Oh," Tina said. In the distance, on the far right side, stood a castle. It looked like a typical fairytale castle made out of dark red brick, with lots of towers, crenulated walls, even a moat.

"Think it's real?" Christine asked. "King Sam didn't list it as one of the true wonders."

"Maybe it isn't in walking distance, can't travel there and back for just a day trip," Tina said. "It would Require the Full Week Package."

Christine giggled.

Good.

Tina needed for Christine's guard to be all the way down.

"So what do you think?" Tina said. "Should we go down to the lake?"

"You sure you want to walk that far?" Christine asked.

"Who said anything about walking?" Tina said as she floated back up off the ground again.

Christine grinned up at her. "Today is a good day, isn't it," she said quietly.

Tina beamed. "The best ever!"

And it would be. Soon.

THE LAKE SMELLED STERILE, AS THOUGH THE COLD and the rocks had killed off anything that might be growing in it. Nothing disturbed the surface, not fish from underneath or the winds now blowing much more strongly around them. The sky remained white overhead, the sun hidden by the peak behind them.

Tina walked right up to the shore. The water seemed sluggish, as if it were filled with mercury. It glowed more brightly as well.

She knelt down and poked a cautious fingertip into the water. It felt viscus and cold, chilling her right to the bone. When she stood and shook her hand, the drops flew everywhere around her, as if she'd stuck her entire fist into the water.

The color of the water cleared.

Instead of being a shiny silver, it was suddenly much darker. Not murky, but a black so shiny it was almost reflective.

It was, Tina realized, the color of her heart.

Seemed that the lake approved of her quest.

"What are you doing?" Christine asked, sounding nervous.

The waters rose up around Tina, forming a type of rail around her. A shield.

They would protect her.

"Did you really think I would just let you take my head?" Tina said.

"What?" Christine squawked. "What are you talking about?"

"You need Tina's head. My head," she said. "Did you really think I was going to just hack my own head off and hand it to you on a silver platter?"

"No," Christine said. "I didn't think I'd need your physical head at all. The pieces I've been collecting have been metaphors. Kind of." She gave a frustrated sigh. "I figured we'd find something here. Something that would represent your head. Not your actual head itself!"

"Right," Tina said. "Maybe you didn't kill the others. They're your *family* after all."

"You're my family, too," Christine said immediately. "My human sister."

"No," Tina said. "We aren't related. We were just tied together through magic."

"Exactly," Christine said. "We are tied together. Closer than blood."

Tina shook her head. "Our Destinies were tied together. Until you stole mine."

"What are you talking about?" Christine asked.

Oh, the stupid troll! She played the part so well.

"You stole my Destiny," Tina reminded her. "Took it so that you could be the great general of the Great War. Well, I'm stealing it back."

"I didn't take your Destiny," Christine said.

Of course she'd deny it.

"I don't need to convince you of that," Tina said. "Though it would be nice if you'd admit the truth."

Before Christine could say anything else, Tina called on all the power she had, all the anger of her betrayal, all the magic she felt in the lake.

She laughed as she brought down a hailstorm of fire on the idiotic troll standing in front of her.

No, Tina didn't need Christine's to admit anything before she died.

CHAPTER TWENTY-ONE

Christine was so shocked at Tina's abrupt betrayal that she nearly didn't get a shield up in time to protect her from the firestorm raining down on her.

"What the hell has gotten into you?" Christine demanded as she blocked Tina's next attack.

Of course, she should have known that things were going too well. Tina had acted happy to see Christine every time she came over. There had only been a couple of times when Christine wondered, when she thought Tina had thrown her a dark, angry look, only to be covered with lighthearted giggles.

How long had Tina been planning this? What was wrong with her? Was she still being influenced by demons? The Zimmermans had been vigilant with their protection spells, particularly once they'd lived with Tina for a few days and came to appreciate just how damaged their daughter had been.

Tina called up dark, billowing smoke—poisonous, if

Christine was taking any bets—and swirled it around the pair of them.

That wasn't one of Tina's normal defenses.

Damn it!

Hell really had gotten its grips on Tina's soul.

How could Christine cleanse it? How could she get those talons out? And not kill Tina, or die herself in the meanwhile?

The water behind Tina appeared to split in two. On the one side, the silver still shone. On the other side, black murky depths raged.

The darkness was gaining on the light.

Christine knew that she only had a little time to save Tina. She had to prevent the dark waters from overtaking the brighter parts.

But how?

And was this why this place was called Soul's Hill? Because the waters of the lake reflected what was truly in one's soul?

Suddenly, Christine knew how to win.

She didn't have to prove that she was a better spellcaster than Tina. While Christine was a mighty fighter, her true skill lay in physical battles, not magical.

No, Christine had to trust that her soul was stronger than Tina's, as it was whole and not divided like her doppelganger's.

She had to make it to the water's edge, though. How?

Tina was intent on driving Christine back, across the rocks and toward the trees.

When Christine glanced over her shoulder, she shuddered at the sight of the prickly vines now waving their branches at her, like a monstrous sea creature. True darkness filled the underside of the trees.

Stepping in there would slick Christine's soul in dark oil, coat it in a shell that would harden, so that she could never escape.

Christine tried to go forward instead. She feinted to the left then tried racing to the right.

Tina wasn't fooled, however. The rain of fire changed into sleeting gouts, flying horizontally, aiming to cut Christine off at the waist.

Damn it. How was Christine going to get around Tina? Make her way to the lake?

Christine tried creating her own storm of fire, behind Tina. Maybe get her to look away from the battle in front of her. Distract her, so that Christine could make a run for it.

But Tina never once looked away. The lake at her back took care of any attack that Christine set up.

Christine even tried throwing boulders at Tina. Even though the rocks here were foreign, Christine still felt enough affinity with them to call them to her, use them to do her will.

Tina cracked open every rock that approached, dissolving them into a rain of dust and gravel. Christine stopped trying to throw boulders quickly as she felt a jolt of pain as each one was destroyed.

Still, Christine wasn't any closer to the water. In fact, she was now a few more steps away from it than she had been.

How could she reach it?

Or did she have to reach it?

Christine called her ax to her hands. She could make out Tina's sneer even through the barrage of magic being tossed her way.

Let Tina underestimate her. Let her believe that Christine was barely capable of defending herself magically and that she needed to attack physically.

With a whooping cry, Christine threw her ax.

Trolls tended to hit whatever it was that they were aiming at, whether it be with stones, darts, or even axes.

The ax flew right over Tina's head, as planned. She tried to knock it to the side, but it just kept traveling.

Diving straight into the waters of the lake itself.

Christine gasped at the cold that suddenly washed over her. She shook her head, letting her own fire element take control for a while, going head-to-head with all the rest of the fire racing around her.

After a few gasping deep breaths, Christine called her ax back, causing it to fly to her hand.

Coated with water.

For a moment, Christine had an image of the state of her own soul. Like Tina's, it had a bright silver edge to it, though hers was tinted with what she thought of as royal troll green.

However, it had a dark edge to it. Much darker than Christine had expected. Christine blamed those on the war, on watching so many good beings die.

She wasn't pure or simple. Not anymore. Never again.

Christine focused on the good parts of her soul. The cleaner parts. The silver that shone with the joy of her family, how good the earth felt under her feet, the smell of fresh dirt, the warmth of a friendly fire.

How, despite the war, there was still goodness to be found, friends and comrades and even mercy.

Christine watched the darkness that covered the lake pause in its ruthless attack of the silver.

"The joy of magic!" Christine called out. "The taste of a good ribeye! The feeling of spring sunshine!"

Tina appeared to have heard Christine. She paused for a moment in her attack, the fire turning to ice around her. "What are you going on about?"

"All the good things you still have in your life," Christine said.

"Right," Tina said. "Remember the joy and all the fun we had and that will get me to forgive you? Not likely."

"But you still have a Destiny!" Christine said, knocking aside the sharp spears of ice that Tina now flung at her.

"You stole it from me!" Tina screamed.

Her face turned a truly impressive shade of red, even through the hail and the storm.

"I did not," Christine said. "That's your doubt talking. It wasn't me. You still have a Destiny. You are meant to fight by my side in the Great War. Hell, you might even win it yourself!"

"I'm meant to lead the armies," Tina said quietly. "Not you."

Christine rolled her eyes. "Then lead," she said.

"What…what do you mean?" Tina asked. "You can't just step back."

"Why the hell not?" Christine said. "I've been waiting for you to get better so that you could join the Great War."

Tina held herself stiffly, as if she'd never even considered that before.

"What about your Destiny?" she asked quietly.

Behind Tina, the silver waters were taking over.

"What about my Destiny?" Christine asked. "According to the oracles, I was supposed to play a large part in the Great War. But so were you. Who the fuck cares if I'm leading the charge or if you are? Just as long as someone does it and puts Lars back in his place. In a prison in Hell."

At the mention of Lars, Tina's head rose up abruptly. "Lars," she hissed, drawing the name out.

"He's the enemy. Not me," Christine said. Again. Why the hell did she have to keep reminding Tina of this simple fact?

Tina gave a great shudder, as if she'd just had a bucket of ice water dumped over her head.

"Lars," she said quietly.

The silver was quickly overtaking the black now.

Tina started floating back toward the ground. "He's been haunting my dreams," she said. She sounded astonished at this.

"Bastard," Christine said. "How?"

Tina gave a great sigh. She carved a space out from next to her.

Christine stiffened and readied her spells. What new tricks would Tina pull on her?

Tina pulled her old wand out of the space.

A wand that, even from a distance, Christine could tell was tainted.

At least Tina didn't immediately wrap her hand

around it, though Christine could tell she was tempted.

"Through this," Tina admitted. "I didn't want to give up my old wand. I didn't, couldn't, see just how badly it had been tainted."

"And now?" Christine asked, still ready to destroy that thing if necessary. She called a small, sharp rock from the ground, floating it up to a ready hand, just in case.

"It's ruined, isn't it?" Tina said.

"It is," Christine told her. "What do you see?"

To Christine, the wand, which looked too much like a prop from one of those popular movies about wizards, had been originally made out of brown wood. Now, the wood looked blackened and brittle, as if it had been burned. She bet that it would splinter at the slightest provocation. Possibly just to be spiteful.

"Black," Tina said. "I can feel it. It's trying to worm its way back into my heart."

"Get rid of it!" Christine said. Her fire element assured her that it could do the job, immolate everything in front of her, if she'd just give it the chance.

Christine didn't want to have to kill Tina. But if her human sister couldn't fight her way free of the demonic influence, Christine might not have a choice.

Tina appeared to be studying Christine from across the way. She nodded, as if she'd finally seen proof of what she was looking for.

She held the wand with her thumb and forefinger, her arm out straight in front of her body.

As she released the wand, it burst into flame. A black, oily smoke rose up from it.

The last of the black waters behind Tina suddenly cleared.

Tina took a deep gulping breath. Then another. And another. She sank down to her knees suddenly, wailing. "I hate being influenced by demons!" she cried.

Christine moved forward cautiously, though she hated herself for not rushing forward to comfort her friend. She couldn't help it, though. She couldn't trust that this wasn't yet another demon trick.

Finally, though, Christine reached Tina's side. She knelt down beside her human sister, wrapping one arm across Tina's back.

Then Christine cried too, for all the lost men, all the lost time, for how much this war had cost everyone.

When they both finished, Christine looked back over the waters.

The silver was still there, though it still appeared to be split in half, part of it pure white, the other tinted royal troll green.

The darkness as still there as well. That was part of being alive in these times. There would always be black places in both of their souls.

Just as long as they didn't let it get the better of them, they'd be okay.

"I have a plan," Tina said slowly. "I know how we can beat him."

For the first time in a very long time, Christine felt the winds of hope stir her own deep waters.

CHAPTER TWENTY-TWO

"Are you sure?" Ty asked. He rocked back on his heels, stunned.

"Got the orders right here," his contact Mandrake said, pulling them out of the tattered leather pouch he had slung over his shoulder and across his chest.

They had met in an alley near Ty's apartment on Capitol Hill. It was one of the neighborhood alleys, not one of the commercial ones, so it had garbage cans neatly lined up next to the garages, not huge industrial dumpsters. The rank smell came from Mandrake, not the surrounding area.

The hot summer sun beat down on their heads, making Ty sweat uncomfortably under his hat. He wore the lightest pants he had—yuppy hiking pants that he'd found at Goodwill, along with a T-shirt and his usual boots.

Mandrake had been playing the part of a homeless man for the last several weeks. He'd carefully ground dirt into his arms and legs before he'd started, to give his skin that "lived in" look. He stank of piss and sweat. Only his eyes were clear, the whites and blue irises startling in his darkened face.

Scraggly hair stuck out from all around Mandrake's head like a mane. He wore a stained and torn muscle-shirt that hung loosely from his skeletal frame, loose brown pants that he held up with a piece of rope, and filthy formerly red sneakers that had no shoelaces.

"Thanks," Ty said, taking the folded paper from Mandrake and looking at it.

Just then, a young white man popped out from between two houses. He looked around carefully, seeing Ty and Mandrake standing just a few feet away. He tried to look casual as he entered the alley, and not as if he'd just been checking everything out. Brown hair flopped over his forehead, covering brown eyes.

He wore the typical uniform of a college kid—oversized purple Huskies T-shirt, long shorts, and sandals. He obviously spent a lot of time in the gym. His shoulders looked oversized compared to his smallish head, and his legs were all muscle. After looking around again, he strolled over to where Ty and Mandrake were standing.

Before the young man could say anything, Ty greeted him. "Hello, officer. What can we do for you?"

Though the disguise was pretty good, Ty could smell the cop on him.

That seemed to startle the kid. Hadn't been undercover for long. "You got any juice?" he still asked.

Ty snorted. "We're not conducting a drug deal here, officer. I'm a private investigator. This is one of my contacts. I am reaching for my wallet now." Ty palmed the paper that Mandrake had given to him and slowly reached into his back pocket, drawing out his wallet. Then he flipped it open to the fake ID he had there, showing that Ty was, in fact, a private investigator.

The guy blew air through his lips loudly. "Pppppppft," he said. "I thought I had something." He looked up eagerly at Ty. "You wouldn't happen to know where they are selling the juice, would you?"

"By juice, I'm assuming you mean the steroids that are being provided to the gym rats up the street?" Ty said, wanting to clarify.

The officer nodded.

"You need to go across the street and the next alley up," Ty said as he put his wallet away. "Ask for Jo. Tall, ginger-haired woman with an attitude problem."

"Ah, thanks," the officer said, nodding at them, then casually strolling on.

"Jo?" Mandrake asked, one eyebrow raised.

Ty grinned at him. "She is, actually, selling drugs. Not so much juice, but speed and cocaine to the stupid jocks around here."

"You wouldn't be naming her just because she's part demon, would you?" Mandrake said with a grin.

"Possibly," Ty said, shrugging. He pulled out the piece of paper that Mandrake had handed to him and unfolded it.

The script was spindly and difficult to read. Of course. Demons had lousy handwriting. And they didn't trust computers, wouldn't use a printer.

The orders were clear, however. All possible troops were being called to a staging area, a pocket world that had been carved out right next to the home of the Risilodan, also known as the rowdy boys.

It appeared that they were going to be the next target of the demons.

"Thank you," Ty said, refolding the paper and handing it back to Mandrake. "I'll let Christine know." He paused, then asked, "You about ready for that bath?"

As part of Mandrake's terms for going this deeply undercover, Ty had agreed to pay for three nights at one of the fancier hotels downtown. The suite Mandrake had picked out had a huge jacuzzi tub that Mandrake had sworn he'd live in for the entire time, or at least until he'd soaked all the dirt and crap out of his skin.

"Not until the war's over, boss," Mandrake told Ty. His blue eyes grew steely. "Not until they're done."

Ty nodded. Mandrake's son had been killed by demons as the result of a party prank gone wrong. Though Mandrake was human and had no magical powers, he still hunted demons whenever he could. Ty had saved his ass when he'd gone after a target who was just too big. After an initial investigation, when Ty had discovered Mandrake's real name and full history, Mandrake had been working for Ty ever since, able to infiltrate places where Ty couldn't go, as Mandrake was fully human.

"Good luck, soldier," Ty said.

"Thanks, boss," Mandrake said.

The older man shook himself. His spine sagged and his posture melted. His expression changed to a leer. Ty would have sworn that the stench from the other man just increased as well. "Got any change?" Mandrake asked, his voice cracking.

Ty snorted at him.

Mandrake gave him a cackling laugh before he turned and shuffled away.

Ty quickly hurried on his way as well. Christine had to know what the demons were planning.

Even if it the note he'd just read was obviously a trap.

CHRISTINE LOOKED EXHAUSTED. SHE'D EVIDENTLY gone straight from her treasure hunt with Tina into a battle. Ty didn't look too closely to see what wounds her human disguise hid.

That she hadn't bothered to hide her tiredness worried him. She was a better illusionist than that.

They sat in the comfortable chairs at the back of one of their favorite spots—a local wine bar. The place had a few good beers on tap—Ty was currently sipping a lovely chocolatey porter—while Christine had opted for a coffee drink that had more alcohol than coffee, at least as far as Ty could smell.

He didn't bother to ask how the war was going. He had a good idea that they were still losing it.

The lights in the bar were low and quiet jazz played on the speakers overhead. As it was a Tuesday night, the place was mostly empty, just a couple of crazy writers in the corner banging away on their keyboards like they were composing angry music, and another woman with an electronic book, reading and sipping wine.

"What news do you have?" Christine asked after a moment.

Even her voice sounded tired.

"Nothing good, I'm afraid," Ty said. "One of my informants was able to steal some orders from a demon. It appears that the next place of attack is going to be the home of the rowdy boys."

"Damn," Christine said. She took another drink of her beverage. "What are the chances that this is a trap?"

Ty smiled grimly. The Christine that he'd first met, who knew nothing about the *kith and kin* or even much about her own trollish nature, would never have come up with such a question.

"Close to one hundred percent," he said. "The message wasn't encrypted in one of the more obscure demon tongues. It was a general call for troops, not something specific. The information was obviously meant to fall into our hands."

Christine nodded. "We haven't lost the war yet, but it's close. Lars knows that I hold the rowdy boys dear. It wouldn't surprise me if Lars also knows that the rowdy boys will turn after a while, ally themselves with the demons. So of course, they are the perfect pressure point for me. To get me to show up with my troops to defend them."

"But why?" Ty asked. "Lars isn't going to be so stupid as to call you out for individual combat, is he?"

After giving him an impressive snort, Christine continued. "He possibly is that egotistical. Thinking that he could beat me in a one-on-one fight."

"Couldn't he?" Ty asked, curious. He knew that Christine was an awesome fighter. Still, Lars was a demon. He was possibly better.

"I could win, if he didn't cheat," Christine said. "And you know demons. They aren't about to play fair. So yes, he would be able to take me because he'd have a trick planned."

"That makes sense," Ty said. "But why focus on you? You have other generals who could take over."

"The *kith and kin* alliance wouldn't hold past my death," Christine said. "They'd fracture. A lot of my allies would turn to the demons."

"How do you win?" Ty asked.

For the first time that evening, Ty saw Christine with a smile. A true smile, not one tainted by exhaustions and haunted by killing.

"With a trick of our own."

CHAPTER TWENTY-THREE

Lars didn't chortle or dance around his office. He was the Supreme General. He had more dignity than that. Honest.

That didn't mean he didn't do a little chair dance wiggle when he got the news. *After* he made sure that he was all alone, no spying eyes peering through the portal on the far wall or tiny spiders from their webs broadcasting Lars' every move. As far as he could tell, it was just him and his parents in the house. The maid was searing something lovely and bloody in the kitchen—Lars had heard the abruptly ended screams of something meaty earlier.

The maps covering the walls of his office had so much more glorious red now. Worlds either taken or destroyed, or enemies who had come crawling back, *kith and kin* who had realigned themselves with their true masters.

And soon…he looked up at the one hole directly behind him. That location where *her* head would be located.

He glanced at the report again. Seemed that a low-level demon had actually taken some initiative and allowed a copy of the plans to be stolen by a simple human, then returned.

Lars had put a lot of A/B testing into the plan language, trying to make sure that it was obscure enough that the enemy would believe the plan, while at the same time not dense enough that the stupid troll wouldn't understand the implications.

Of course, if Christine actually bothered to go to the location where Lars was supposedly gathering his troops, she'd be in for a rude surprise.

As in "hot lava in the old town tonight" sort of surprise.

While Lars knew that the enemy was nowhere near as clever as him and his demon generals, he did know that Christine wasn't actually stupid.

Underestimating the enemy was what had gotten him into trouble more than once. Along with most of the demons he knew.

So he had his contingency plans ranked, depending on if the enemy was dumb, smart, or even smarter.

Christine was sure to take the bait. She'd show up in the world of the rowdy boys with an army for certain.

He also knew that she probably would be smart enough to understand that this was a trap.

She'd never be able to guess what he'd had planned for her…

The question was merely a matter of time. Would she send her armies ahead of her? Mass them in another pocket and come pouring in to the rescue? Or would she wait until the battle was well underway before she showed up?

Lars was prepared for every contingency.

As for that damned obelisk of truth that she was supposedly assembling—no one had any idea of what exactly that was. Or what it was supposed to do. The humans had the best oracles of all the races. Lars was a big enough demon to admit that seeing the future was really not a strong suit of demons.

Plus, he had no idea what the hell she'd do with it once she did assemble it. Would it allow her some great magical boon? Something she could fight him with? Allow her to see through every trap he set? That might get sticky.

Still, even without his tricks and traps, Lars knew that he could kill her. He had more than one recording of her fighting, now, and had studied her every move.

She was good. He could admit that. She'd gotten much better over the last five years.

He was still better. Particularly now that he knew his enemy so well.

Soon, he'd have her head on his wall. The Great War would be won a few weeks after that, when the last of her pathetic resistance had died.

Then Lars would be crowned one of the princes of Hell. He had plans for how to survive both until then, as well as after that.

CHAPTER TWENTY-FOUR

Vern gratefully slid into his car. He folded forward, reaching his arms over his steering wheel and stretching out his back. He wasn't used to standing for hours. Then he took the time to stretch out his cramped hands.

Goodness! Trying to gather signatures for the upcoming vote on funding the *kith and kin* and the war had taken a lot out of him. More than he'd expected.

Though part of his exhaustion came from standing there with a clipboard unable to even catch the eye of most people. They wouldn't even say hello! As if he was some sort of pariah. It made him resolve to say hello to everyone from now on.

At least he had gathered quite a few signatures. He didn't know if it was enough.

How could they think about cutting off all support for Christine and the war? He just didn't get it. It was so short sighted on their part. He'd had an ugly feeling that part of it was the "human first" movement, which had to be influenced by demons, he swore.

Vern cricked his neck from one side to the other, trying to work out the kinks. He rolled his head, then took a deep breath and sighed.

Though it was after eight, he just couldn't go home yet. He was too wound up still. If he went home now, all he'd end up doing would be to angrily pace the living room floor. And Lizzie had had enough of his rants for now, quite frankly.

While Vern liked to think of himself as a youngster at heart, he really didn't want to go to a bar, particularly not the type of bar that would be for old farts like him.

Where else could he go? He'd discovered that he really enjoyed being outdoors more as his magic had come to the forefront. Something invigorating about striving to produce your own strong blowing wind, facing off against a storm. Though there hadn't been any storms that summer. He still could well imagine it.

There had been those reports about demons coming across the fairy bridge that Christine maintained. She'd assured him that it wasn't possible. He believed her.

Still, it wouldn't hurt for him to go and check it out on his own.

Vern took a deep breath then reminded himself that he needed to *pay attention*. Even Lizzie had complained about his driving recently. There was just so much more to see!

Still, Vern made himself check behind his vehicle twice before he backed out of his parking spot, then look both ways twice before he pulled out into the street.

It was a short drive down Madison Street to the Arboretum. Vern reminded himself a couple of times to pay attention to the traffic, not marvel at the new buildings going up, the loud thumping music of the car beside his, the smell of the night, sweet and wild.

Vern pulled into the parking lot beside the Japanese garden. He sagged with relief that he'd gotten there unscathed.

Concentrating so hard on his driving made him tired. Maybe he was going to have to give up his car…

Just not yet.

Vern got out. The night air instantly revived him. He looked in all directions. He'd never had good night vision before, but his magic had improved his eyesight tremendously.

Nothing dangerous lurked close to him. Something was camped out behind him, in the ravine at the edge of the park. He didn't know what, but it was a passive evil, not active. It probably wouldn't come up and bother his car.

Still, Vern pressed his hand against the side window. A brief flare of blue told him that the car was now sheltered in a protection spell. It wouldn't last too long, it wasn't as if he was enchanting the object. That would take a lot of time, ingredients, as well as skill. It wasn't necessary to go to that extreme. Just a short protection spell would do.

Humming, Vern walked across the parking lot, then across the street and into the park. The bridge was located in the southern part of the Arboretum, spanning across a dried riverbed. Only in the spring after really heavy rains did the river have any water in it.

The air smelled so good, fresh with the winds and the night. Vern felt his nervous energy bleeding away, carried from him by the breezes surrounding him.

He was going to have to remember this, how good it felt to walk at night. Maybe this was what he needed to start doing—walking in the evenings around the lake.

Or maybe there was a neighborhood watch he could join, and he'd walk the blocks around his house, making sure his neighborhood was safe and protected.

Vern shivered when the air changed and a foul smell washed over him.

Without thinking about it, Vern automatically put up a distraction spell. It wouldn't necessarily turn him invisible. However, unless someone was actually looking for him, their eyes would slide across him and not register that he was there. He'd found that it was the best defense when faced with a demon or three.

And there were suddenly more than three demons in front of him.

Luckily, they weren't paying any attention to Vern. They'd materialized on the far side of the bridge, the human side. He hadn't seen them cross, however.

What was going on?

Vern took a few more steps toward the bridge, peering carefully at it.

A blur of white passed over the top of it.

What the hell?

Vern stayed where he was and *focused*, trying to see exactly what was happening.

There.

A bent over white figure was racing across the bridge.

On its back, it bore a demon.

Only when the creature reached the far end of the bridge did Vern realize what was happening.

The white figure was a cambion, half human, half demon. It carried a full demon on its back.

That was how the demons were getting across the bridge. They were probably using the same technique to enter the other worlds as well.

Why were the cambions able to cross the bridge? Was it because they were half human? That was the only thing that Vern could figure out. The bridge itself was barred against oath breakers. Maybe these were particularly harmless cambions?

Vern's palm itched. He really wanted to pull out his wand and challenge these demons, stop them from coming any further into the human plane.

However, he was by himself. A single human, facing a group of two dozen demons.

He'd never survive. He just wasn't strong enough on his own.

Disappointed, Vern slipped away, unnoticed.

Could he use the parade of demons entering the human plane as evidence that they needed to help the *kith and kin*?

No, the opposition would take it as proof of the failure of the *kith and kin*, how they needed to take matters in their own hands, to not trust the others.

Humans first.

Vern shuddered.

The stench of demons now surrounded Vern's car. He could tell that they'd tested the spell. It had blackened in areas, near the driver's door, across the front window.

No, that wasn't all they'd done.

They'd actually shit on his car.

Because they couldn't damage it magically, they'd done the next best thing. At least according to them.

Damn them. Damn them all!

Vern's anger bubbled up. He was so tired of this. So tired of watching the war bleed the life out of his daughter. Tired of the arguments between his own people when they should have been united, fighting the true enemy and not each other. Tired of feeling useless, as though there wasn't anything he could do.

It took a lot to get Vern angry. He prided himself on always being a pacific kind of guy, easy going.

This was too much.

Vern's wand found its way to his hand without him willing it.

He *blasted* the car with bright blue flames, burning away the last of the demon stench.

Now he saw the ropes that the demons had tried to tie to the car. Thin lines of influence and power.

What were those? Were the demons so intent on influencing him that they'd attacked his vehicle? Since they couldn't get through to him or his family?

Vern burned through those as well, unsure when they'd been first attached.

He thought he heard a yelp in the distance as he followed the lines back, burning brightly as they went, streams of hot fire flashing though the black night.

Damn them all.

When he was finished, the car was as clean as if it had just come from the wash.

However, Vern's anger still burned, white hot now.

He'd had enough. Enough of the politics and being friendly and trying to persuade others to his side.

Time to go and kick some demon ass.

CHAPTER TWENTY-FIVE

"Where did these come from?" the royal treasurer, Phikathera, asked suspiciously.

"Does it matter?" King Garethen growled. "It's gold. Spend it."

Phikathera shook her head. It was late in the evening, when proper trolls were either out drinking or possibly already passed out. Phikathera wore a more casual outfit, merely a tight fitting vest made out of a rich brown and gold material, showing off her clear olive skin and her bright white tusks.

They were meeting in the king's private study. He'd brought in two of the chests of gold coins that Manny the demon had given him. Though the king had set winds to stir the gold, they still might have had the slightest stench of demon.

Maybe he should have come up with a story about stealing the chests from the demons.

Too late now.

The chests were made of wood and reinforced with

iron bands, about two feet long, one foot wide and one foot deep. Gold coins filled each chest to the brim. The top locked with a magical device that was set to the king's own thumbprint—a technology that he would swear the humans had copied.

They were extremely heavy. However, not too heavy for a troll to lift. Particularly when aided with magic.

Phikathera drew up a handful of the coins and inspected them. "They're real," she commented after a moment.

"What, did you think I would try to pay my own troops with false gold?" King Garethen roared. How dare she doubt him?

Phikathera speared him with a look. Her dark brown eyes sparked with a deep fire. "This gold came from the demons," she said bluntly. "How did you acquire it?"

"I stole it," the king lied. He could tell that the treasurer didn't believe him. "What does it matter?" he asked again. "I'm giving it to you to help fund the war effort."

It had cost the king greatly to hand over the chests, though he still had over a dozen more stashed in his private vault. However, the war wasn't going their way. The *kith and kin* weren't desperate. Not yet. But they were only a few lost battles away from that. The latest meeting that King Garethen had had with Ozlandia the head of the guard had warned of just how badly things were going.

"I will use this gold," Phikathera said, turning slowly to face the king. "Despite its questionable…heritage."

At least she didn't say *source*, as it had come from him, though Garethen could tell she'd wanted to.

"See that it's well spent," King Garethen commanded.

Phikathera snorted. "First, I will see that it's well cleaned. Then I will worry about spending it wisely." She cast a shrewd eye at him. "Are there more where these came from?"

"Why?" the king asked, unwilling to give this woman even an inch.

"I could have used them earlier," she said simply. "Now, I'm just hoping that it isn't too late."

After Phikathera left, King Garethen sat in his heavy chair behind his good stone desk, brooding. Should he have turned over the gold chests to the treasurer when he'd first received them? But it was *his* gold! He shouldn't have to fund the entire war effort on his own. There was plenty of gold in the treasury for that.

He should have started taxing the merchants sooner, making them pay for the war effort.

How could Garethen get the coins back? He already felt the loss of them, the place of honor where the chests had sat a bothersome hole, like a missing a tooth that his thoughts kept circling around.

It was too late to change his mind and take the chests back.

But maybe he could raise taxes again…

CHAPTER TWENTY-SIX

Nik was just about to shut down the portal, to mark his shop as "Closed" for the night, when Christine came walking in.

"Ah," Nik said. "I was expecting you."

Normally, seeing Christine always made Nik happy.

Tonight, he couldn't help but feel sad.

He flipped the portal sign to "Closed" anyway—he didn't want anyone coming in during the middle of this confrontation.

Nik had been wearing his most comfortable clothes the last few days, mainly plaid flannel shirts, carefully tailored jeans, and his expensive, handmade leather shoes. Today, he wore his dark blue and black flannel that had been washed the perfect number of times, making it soft and warm. Despite the fact that Nik rarely felt cold or heat.

Christine wore her armor, all set for battle in her chainmail, with her ax on her back. She didn't have her helmet on, but Nik knew that she could grab it quickly if she needed it.

She also appeared in her full troll guise, nearly eight feet tall, with sharp tusks and muscled arms. The scars on her arms stood out that evening, blazing white against her greenish skin.

She'd withstood hellfire as a baby.

What hope did Nik have that she wouldn't bring all of her considerable powers to bear on him in order to get the thing she needed most of all right now?

Christine stepped forward. The lights came up brightly, much brighter than what Christine generally liked for shopping.

It took Nik a moment to realize that this amount of light was what Christine preferred during a battle.

"How long have you known that your mirror was the final piece of the obelisk of truth?" Christine asked as she continued to walk down the aisle of goods, such wonderful items that Nik had always treasured.

Nik shrugged. "I didn't know for certain, not at first. And I wasn't about to say anything until I was absolutely sure. You know that."

Christine nodded. "I do. I've never understood why, though."

Nik bobbed his head from one side to the other, thinking. Should he tell her his story? That because he'd been so influenced by demons when he'd been human, he vowed to never speak on any topic until he'd thoroughly researched it to make sure that what he was saying was true, and not a lie someone else had magically put into his head?

"Bad things happened a long time ago because I spoke out of turn," Nik finally said. "I learned my lesson."

No one alive needed to know the depths of his betrayal of his own race, the guilt he'd never gotten over, even though intellectually he knew that it hadn't been his fault.

"So why didn't you come to me when you did know?" Christine asked quietly.

Nik gave a bitter laugh. Funny, he'd never thought of himself capable of such nuanced expression before.

"I'd been warned off," Nik said.

"By who?" Christine growled.

He could tell that she was ready to go and do battle for him. All he had to do was to point her in a direction. But he could never tell her the truth.

Not her. Not anyone.

"It doesn't matter," Nik said. He'd also debated telling her the truth of her actions, his actions. He'd finally decided that it wouldn't be fair if he didn't give her the choice.

He took a deep breath, though he didn't really breathe anymore. Not like that.

"Giving you the mirror, even if I make you pay dearly for it, would break my neutrality," he said. "I would be seen to be favoring one side of the Great War over another."

"That's stupid," Christine said. "I've been set on a quest by the oracles. Why should that put your neutrality into question?"

"Because I know the consequences of my actions," Nik said. "If I give you the mirror, there's a good chance you'll win the war. I can't guarantee it. However, if I don't give you the mirror, you'll lose. You have no chance."

"Okay," Christine said slowly. "That sucks. What happens to you if lose your neutrality?"

Nik gave her a sad smile. "I wasn't born in this body," he said. He held out his hands, manipulating the fine wooden joints of his fingers. "I made it. And then I had my consciousness transferred from my old body to this new one."

"Why?" Christine asked. She took a step forward, obviously fascinated.

Nik didn't want to tell her his story. But if anyone should know, it should be Christine. "I was born human," he said, raising his chin defiantly. "And I was corrupted by demons without realizing it."

It was his greatest regret, that he'd been so stupid, so arrogant, that he'd believed himself above all taint.

"This body can't be influenced," Nik continued. "But I couldn't make the transfer on my own. I had to call in a favor. The being who performed the magic made my neutrality part of my agreement. If I remained neutral and sold magic items to all beings who desired them, I would be sustained. I could stay in this body forever. Once I break my neutrality, our deal is over."

"Wait a minute," Christine said. "You're going to die if you give me the mirror?" She looked absolutely horrified.

"I would like to tell you that I don't know for certain, to ease this blow. But I cannot," Nik said. "I won't lie to you. Yes, I believe that if I give you the mirror, I will cease to exist."

"I won't take it," Christine said hotly. "I won't be responsible for your death."

Nik shook his head. "Think about it. If you refuse the mirror, you will lose. The demons will win the Great War. Everything you've done up until now, everything you've fought for, all the lives already lost, will be for naught."

Christine still looked horrified.

"Your family will die. All your friends. The earth as you know it will perish," Nik said, pressing his point home. "It is a single sacrifice for the greatest good. You know that it's the right thing to do."

"It isn't fair," Christine whispered. Tears had started running down her cheeks. "I don't want to do this."

"I know," Nik said. At least he couldn't join her crying. "But you have to. War forces terrible choices upon us."

"You're sure, you're absolutely sure, that the demons will win the Great War if I don't take the mirror?" Christine asked as she wiped the tears away from her face with the backs of her hands.

"Yes," Nik said. He felt the truth of what he said down deep inside himself. Though he didn't have bones, the words still resonated that way. Maybe it was through the grain of his wooden body.

"Oh, gods, Nik," Christine breathed out. "You know I would rather do anything at all, anything else, than to cause you harm."

Nik nodded, then gave her a brave smile. "Maybe they'll let me set up shop someplace else. It's all I've ever loved, running this shop."

Christine gave him a watery giggle. "Nik's Heavenly Emporium?" she guessed.

"Maybe," Nik said, smiling at the thought. Then he sobered. "It was my privilege and my honor to work with you."

Christine gave an audible gulp. "Mine as well." She held out her hand.

Normally, Nik didn't touch anyone. But for just this once, he reached across the counter and wrapped his fingers around Christine's burning hot hand, giving it a gentle squeeze.

Then, before he could back out, Nik reached into a personal pocket of space and pulled out the mirror.

He'd left the lace doily across the face of it.

The antique porcelain base looked tiny and frail in Christine's huge palm. The gold rising from the base and encircling the mirror itself suddenly gained a polished gleam.

"Don't," he warned Christine before she pulled the cover from the mirror. "Leave it until you're ready to set it into the obelisk itself." There wasn't any reason why she couldn't look in the mirror, but Nik wanted her to wait. Mainly because the mirror would show Christine her true self, and he was worried what she might see, having just agreed to kill him.

"I cannot tell you how much taking this breaks my heart," Christine said, holding the mirror as if it were the greatest treasure she'd ever encountered.

"Me, too," Nik said.

A deep tone sounded through Nik's entire body. It was as if the bell that he'd set up that told him that a customer had come through the portal had been amplified one thousand percent. He was surprised that it hadn't shaken the walls themselves.

"You need to go. Now," he said.

Christine gave him a puzzled look.

"Now!" Nik shouted. He didn't want Christine to have to witness what was coming.

"I will always remember you, my friend," she said. Tears poured down her face. Then she turned and raced out of the sanctuary of the store.

Nik knew he only had seconds.

Luckily, he'd prepared for this.

The shelves started to empty themselves. Ingredients flew toward the various waiting portals that suddenly sprang up along the far wall.

He was giving his entire stock to the humans and others who were fighting the war against the demons. Plus instructions for how to counter some of the worst of the spells the demons were casting, that he'd supplied ingredients for.

Svetlana didn't make her appearance until the final shelf had been cleared.

"I see you've been busy," she said, looking around the room. While the shelves remained, everything else had vanished. Even the posters had been sent back to the manufacturers. The lights glared down, as bright as the noonday sun in the desert. Instead of smelling faintly of incense and warm velvet, the shop had a baked scent, like hot rock.

Nik raised his chin defiantly. "I knew the time was coming," he said. "That you would come for me for breaking my neutrality."

"Which is why I waited until you were finished distributing everything," Svetlana told him with a smile. Her gray robes seemed a little brighter that day. Though for some reason, her golden hair seemed a bit off, like it had been dyed the wrong shade of blonde.

"Are you ready?" Svetlana said. A tall sword sprang up in her hands. Though she held the shaft of it close to her waist, the tip of it rose far above her head, covered in glowing white flames.

"I am," Nik said. He stepped from around the counter for the last time, facing the angel.

Instead of violently swinging the sword and removing his head, as Nik had expected, Svetlana tenderly lowered the blade until it kissed his shoulder, like a queen knighting a beloved champion. Then she swung it around and touched his other shoulder.

It didn't hurt. Not exactly. It was more like a surprising heat shooting through him, like being touched by a hot iron that abruptly cooled.

Nik's body trembled. He shook his head, trying to clear it.

He felt himself rise up, following the sword as Svetlana pulled it away.

No, just his consciousness rose up.

His little wooden body that had served him so well for centuries tumbled to the ground, like a marionette whose strings had just been cut.

Nik was surprised that he was still aware. "What happens next?" he said. Or he tried to say. Somehow, he managed to communicate the thought as he rose up through the ceiling, flying after Svetlana.

He felt, rather than saw, the brilliant smile. "Someone is waiting for you. Has been, for the longest time."

They reached a different plane, traveling from the human night to this new place in the blink of an eye, without using a portal.

Damned angels. How did they do that?

This place wasn't well formed. Nik felt the potential, however. It felt raw, not sterile but barren. Just waiting for the right seed to take hold. It seemed to be primarily made of rocks and ice, sentient fog and dripping water.

A figure rose up in front of Nik.

He gasped.

The being—no, human—had Nik's face. His old face. The one he'd been born with, the one that he'd looked at occasionally in the mirror of truth. Dark hair and brooding eyes, thin lips with a sharp smile.

The human held his arms open.

Nik had no choice but to rush forward, to be reunited with the rest of his soul. He felt himself sink into the human body. Except it wasn't a body. Not really. It was merely a vase to hold his full being.

Whole for the first time in centuries, Nik turned to face Svetlana.

He gasped as the blonde wig flew off and the true nature of the angel was revealed.

Finally. He remembered.

Svetlana. His former wife. The one whom he'd betrayed and killed because of the influence of the demons.

He discovered that the shell his soul wore could cry in this place.

"Are you finally ready to join me?" Svetlana asked. Her voice held the terrible warnings that only an angel could manage, along with warmth and glad tidings.

Nik sighed. He'd stayed on earth to try to make up for the horrible things he'd done during the last Great War. He knew that he'd made a difference, despite the promise of neutrality that he'd upheld.

There was still so much to do.

However, it was now someone else's turn to do it.

"I am," Nik said.

He stepped forward, reaching for the angel's outstretched hand.

Together they flew off as Nik grew his wings and left all things human behind.

CHAPTER TWENTY-SEVEN

"How the heck does this thing go together?" Christine groused as she looked at the scattered pieces of the obelisk of truth.

She'd set them out on the floor of her living room once she could finally face looking at the mirror again. She didn't have the time to mourn Nik and his sacrifice properly. Still, she'd given herself a single night. Now, in the morning, she needed to forge ahead.

She promised herself that she'd grieve for him properly later.

She didn't know if she'd ever be able to forgive herself, however. Causing his death cut her more deeply than any of the other souls she'd condemned.

Damn this war. Damn Lars and his demons.

Christine knew she didn't have much time. There were already too many rumors of *kith and kin* races meeting with the demons, possibly signing pacts with them, switching sides, preparing to come and storm the human plane.

She sat cross-legged on the good solid dirt of her living space. It gave her some comfort, as it always did. She wore a simple shirt and yoga pants, hoping to feel comfortable in her skin, though she doubted that would occur for a long, long time. Books surrounded her, still the balm of her soul. She'd fixed her favorite coffee that morning, then added heavy cream, vanilla, and honey. Yum.

She picked up the vase, Vern's vase, supposedly the base of the obelisk. It was small and frail, a child's creation. How could it possibly support the huge statue that was Dennis' torso? She knew that if she tried to rest the heavy marble on top of the delicate porcelain, it would shatter.

Then there was Tina's head. Mostly, that had turned out to be metaphorical, as Tina had had to get her head straightened out before she could help Christine and the war.

Still, they'd needed some physical object, some memento of their visit to the Sammuthians. They couldn't take the entire lake with them. Tina had tried dipping a stone in the water, seeing if it would cling appropriately, coat the rock as it had coated her hand, but that didn't work either.

Finally, after being scolded by King Sam for despoiling the natural setting by trying to take a rock with them, they were escorted to the gift shop.

Tina was instantly drawn to a snow globe that showed the lake and the mountains. It was about a foot tall, a thick glass ball sitting on top of a cherry wood square base. When she shook it, the silver flakes glowed brightly as they swirled, before the slowly floated back down.

So—Tina's head. At least Tina had made the joke

about how empty it had seemed before Christine (or someone else) did.

Then there was Nik's mirror. Christine had left it covered as he'd requested. She wanted to flick the white lace doily away, but she restrained herself.

It had been one of his last requests. She would honor that, even when her soul told her that there was no need.

She hadn't tried pinging the store that morning. She didn't want to be confronted with the truth of his death. Not yet. In her mind, he could still be alive, stocking the shelves of the emporium, waiting on customers, taking delight in a hard bargain.

Where did the mirror go? In the center of the piece? How was she supposed to attach it? Did it go on the top? How the hell was she supposed to balance the mirror on top of the round snow globe?

Christine called up her air power, seeing if it had heard any hints or rumors about how to assemble this thing, but it had no idea either.

Using her magic, Christine floated all the objects up off the ground. Holding them there, she could assemble them in the order they belonged.

But they didn't magically weld themselves together, didn't flow or mold themselves into an actual obelisk. That only happened in Hollywood movies.

Christine let the pieces settle back down onto the ground again. She picked up the map she had sitting beside her. It didn't show her anything new. Every time she'd found a piece, an animation would spring up, showing her the next piece, giving her its name and where it was located.

Now that she had all the pieces assembled together, whatever magic the map had once held had flowed out of the world.

What was she supposed to do? Who would know? It wouldn't be Tina, that much Christine realized. Tina had been instrumental in collecting the pieces. She wasn't supposed to put them together.

Tina had come up with a brilliant plan for how Christine was going to display the obelisk to her troops.

If Christine could ever fit the damned thing together.

Who else was left? Ty had already helped her find the various worlds. She doubted her bio-dad would be able to help. Maybe she could go back to the oracles? No, that didn't feel right either.

Christine took a last sip of her coffee. Damned, that was good.

She couldn't stay here, though, buried in her comfortable home. She had to figure this out.

Who did she know who was good at puzzles?

She tried to dismiss the thought that came instantly to her mind.

But it remained.

Mum.

"Hello, dear," Mum said, coming over to the table where Christine sat, arms held out.

Christine didn't like to hug or touch anyone. Particularly not a human. That was just part of her innate troll nature.

She still accepted a mum hug gladly, realizing just how much she'd missed that.

"I'm so glad that you called and wanted to do lunch today," Mum said. She sat down gracefully in her chair, then reached out and took her daughter's hand, squeezing it. "No business before ordering," she added sternly.

Christine grinned at her. "Got it," she said, picking up her own menu.

She'd chosen a restaurant close to her mum's office. It was strictly a human place, as far as Christine could tell. Still, she was going to have to come back here, and probably bring Ty, as this place served MEAT. She could order it by the slice, or by the quarter, half, or whole pound. The entire room smelled of the charcoal grill they had going in the kitchen.

The side dishes all looked yummy, including homemade sweet potato tatter tots and brussel sprouts grilled with honey and bacon.

After ordering a sampler of both appetizers as well as meats and sauces, Christine took a deep breath.

"You go first," Mum said, obviously reading the impatience of her daughter.

"Thanks," Christine said. "I have a puzzle to put together now. All the pieces that go into the obelisk of truth. But I can't figure out how to assemble it." She tried to keep the low growl out of her voice.

"They don't magically fit together?" Mum asked.

Christine shook her head. "Nope. Or physically," she added.

"Tell me about the pieces," Mum said.

So Christine explained about the vase, the sculpture,

the snow globe, and the mirror. She didn't mention that Nik was dead. That wound was still too fresh.

Mum realized that there was something wrong as Christine went on to describe the mirror, reaching out to squeeze her daughter's arm, though she didn't interrupt.

"The pieces must have a theme," Mum said after a moment. "What do all the pieces mean, emotionally, to you?"

Christine blinked, surprised. Mum wasn't really the touchy-feely type. She'd generally had to be the practical parent, given her dad's frequent flights of fancy.

"Dad's vase—he said it was a father's pride," Christine said quietly. It still filled her with quiet stillness, to feel Dad's love that way. "Dennis's statue is all about being 'born ready,'", Christine said. She couldn't help but roll her eyes. She thought for a moment. "Dennis is my big brother. Maybe he was 'born ready' to take care of his little sister."

Mum nodded her encouragement. "So how do those fit together?" she asked.

Christine shrugged. "They've got me in common, I guess." But she still didn't see how they all fit.

"So tell me about Tina," Mum said.

Christine gave Mum the abbreviated version, about how Tina had been influenced by demons to the point where she'd thought that Christine had stolen her Destiny.

"But she's finally free from all influence," Christine said. She was aware that while that was technically true, the repercussions of that influence were likely to be around for a while.

"As you said before, Tina's head is now clear," Mum said. "As clear as that glass ball."

"And she's ready to fight. She has her magic back," Christine said. She had sympathized so much with Tina's plight as she still remembered when her own magic had been blocked, split apart and held separately.

"She's ready to fight for you," Mum corrected gently.

"It isn't all about me," Christine said uncomfortably.

Mum merely raised an eyebrow in Christine's direction.

"It isn't. It can't be," Christine insisted, though now she was starting to wonder.

"And what did Nik give you?" Mum asked after a moment.

"Nik gave me everything," Christine said, her voice suddenly cracking. "Don't—don't ask about it. Not yet," she warned, holding her hand up.

"I see," Mum said. "I'm sorry," she added. She looked as though she wanted to give her daughter a hug, but she wasn't about to reach across the table to do so.

A father's pride. A brother's support. The clear vision of her friends. And the willingness to lay down their lives for her. To stop this war.

Suddenly, Christine saw her mistake.

The pieces were, in fact, not for her. She already had these things. The obelisk of truth merely let her realize her own resources, the depths of her support. She didn't need to find them.

The obelisk would only assemble itself for those who needed it. The demoralized troops. The *kith and kin* races that had been corrupted by the demons. Even the humans who were suffering from demonic influence.

They were the ones who needed to see the truth.

Christine and Tina had already come up with a plan for how to survive the coming attack by Lars, and how Christine would escape from the trap he'd so carefully laid.

It wouldn't take much modification for Christine to be able to assemble the obelisk, hold the pieces ready, for her troops to view.

"Thank you," Christine said finally. She was aware that she'd been "away" for a while, figuring out her victory.

"You're welcome," Mum said. She sighed. "Are you sure that you have the pieces now? That you have a winning game plan?"

Christine nodded. "I think I do. As Nik said, there's no guarantee that we will win. But I think we have a fighting chance finally."

"Good," Mum said firmly.

She pressed her lips together as if she wanted to say more.

"What is it?" Christine said. Mum had seemed really eager to meet her for lunch. What was going on?

Mum sighed. "It's your father," she said finally. "I've been fine with him merely gathering names and going to political caucuses, raising support for you and your armies. But war is fought by young men and women, being directed by older, wiser heads. Not by old soldiers."

"What do you mean?" Christine said, confused. That certainly seemed like an accurate description of human warfare. *Kith and kin* fought together, young and old alike.

"Your father has decided to join the army," Mum said. "Your army. He's going to get himself killed."

"No," Christine said. "I won't let him."

"Too late. He's already joined up."

Christine cursed under her breath. Though given the look Mum just shot her, she hadn't said it quietly enough.

"I'll stop him," Christine said. Though she wasn't exactly sure how.

Mum shook her head. "You can't stop him. He's made up his mind. Just protect him. Bring him back home alive."

Though it made Christine's soul ache to the very core of her being, all she could say was, "I'll try." She couldn't promise to keep him alive. It was war, after all.

And even if he did come back with all his fingers and toes, Christine knew that wasn't enough. War would change her dad, like it had changed her. She could protect his physical body. But she couldn't protect his soul.

How could she get him to turn away from this course? Could she stop him? Or was the war going to destroy her entire family?

CHAPTER TWENTY-EIGHT

BUDDY STAMPED HIS APPROVAL ON THE FINAL WAR plans that the Supreme General had submitted to the Ultimate General. The bloody ink gave a satisfying squishing sound. Buddy had had the stamp made up just to approve war plans. It was at least six inches long and three inches wide, obscuring the print below it. His PR department had consulted with him on the design, recommending the huge, bloody thing. It was one of the ways he could divert attention away from the creator of the plan back to himself.

However, Buddy was aware that his approval was literally just a rubberstamp at this point. Even without his approval, Lars would go ahead with his plans.

Buddy had considered withholding his approval. That way, if Lars failed, Buddy would have an additional fallback plan and could disassociate himself from the disaster more easily.

The last few weeks had taught Buddy how to plan better. He'd actually learned more about planning from

Lars. Buddy was a big enough demon to admit that—to himself, when he was all alone in his office. Never out loud or in front of anyone else.

He had a reputation to maintain.

If Lars failed, it would take Buddy a while to regain his standing among the princes of Hell. The rest of the cowards would be sure to blame Buddy for all their grievances.

And Buddy had plans for them as well.

In the meanwhile, Buddy would go along with what Lars had planned. Christine was merely a troll. They weren't known for being sneaky. Or even that smart. She'd fall for Lars' schemes, expose herself and her troops, and would fall.

And when she fell, all the worlds would fall.

Sure, there would be some hanger-oners, the ones who would keep fighting after their general was defeated. They wouldn't last long.

And then…and then! Buddy couldn't help but get up from behind his desk and waggle his butt around, doing a hopping dance that had yet to catch on with the cool kids. He waved his arms in the air and shook his tail.

And then Lars would know his true place in the scheme of things. He wouldn't be able to resist the charms of Curly.

Buddy was sure to come out on top. He always did.

CHAPTER TWENTY-NINE

Lars looked out from his perch, high above the demon camps. He reclined on a long couch in his full demon form, all long and snaky. The struts that made up his wings had been polished by a bone smith just the night before, all the spikes on his tail were razor sharp, and he'd even drunk a bit of caustic human soda in his demon form, to insure that the acid of his spit was particularly corrosive.

Tents and barracks stretched out from the rock mountain Lars sat on to the horizon. The smell of cooking fires and rangy demons made Lars' heart sing.

So many demons from all over had been assembled for him! Earlier that afternoon, he'd sat on his perch and let representatives from each group parade before him.

Not all of the demons would bow down to him. Demons were touchy about lowering their heads. But they would see the brilliance of Lars and would kneel. Particularly once Lars decisively won this battle. All demons on all the planes would hold him in awe.

His planning was flawless. He didn't have a single plan, but multiple contingencies, because no single plan survived contact with the enemy.

By the end of this battle, Lars was going to have Christine's head on a plaque behind his desk.

The world would fall and the demons would be on top, the natural order of things restored.

"Sir!" One of the demon generals came bouncing up to where Lars sat. It was Moe, Lars realized after a moment. The demon's armor strained around his pudgy middle, the strings holding the chainmail corset together frayed. He wore a helmet stolen from the trolls, with a peaked ridge running down the center. His ax looked sturdy and well used.

"The enemy has just landed a huge force in the home world of the rowdy boys," Moe said with glee. "I wanted to be the one to personally tell you the news."

Only then did Lars notice the blood that still dripped from Moe's ax. Had he killed the original messenger? Possibly. It was a good thing that demons could reproduce quickly and were naturally fearsome fighters, or Lars might have worried more about the in-troop fighting.

"Is Christine with them?" Lars asked, sliding to the front of the long couch he reclined on.

"She is! She is!" Moe said, bobbing his head up and down, his entire body shaking as though it were composed of a thick gelatin. "Should I alert the shock troops?"

Lars considered for a moment. "No," he said slowly. "We're going with plan 4B, subsection 16."

Moe screwed up his face in concentration. "Was that the one where we don't send the shock troops in?"

Lars sighed. It was so hard to get good help these days, even with all the competition among his generals for the top ranks. No one had his head for plans.

"We send the shock troops. And the secondary troops. But we hold back the primary troops until later."

"Oh, yes, I see," Moe said, bobbing again.

"I'll alert the troops," Lars said dryly. The only way to make sure that things got done right was to do it himself, sometimes.

Christine wouldn't be expecting wave after wave of demon forces all coming to attack.

As well as his other surprises.

LARS (AND A COUPLE OF OTHER GENERALS WHO could fly) floated above the field of battle, spying on the enemy.

He had to admit that he wasn't expecting Christine's troops to be so well dug in. Had she been assembling them secretly for a while? It took him a moment to realize that all the earth foundations were new and had been dug by the trolls.

Generally, the *kith and kin* didn't work together like that. Each army was separate and fought on their own.

Huh.

He'd have to take that into account the next time he battled with a group of *kith and kin*. Though there weren't likely to be any other battles as big as this one.

Still, he could put it in his memoirs. He'd already started writing those. He knew it was a useless exercise.

The twelve volume set he had planned would only be used as punishment for younger demons coming up.

But he hoped that he would influence at least one or two young demons along the way. The ones who were smart enough to see how useful a plan could be.

The swelling roar of his troops washed over Lars like a lullaby, giving him goosebumps all across his shoulders, under his scales. Though this wasn't a time for sleep, but a time to commit the art of war.

"Charge!" Lars heard the calls and the discordant horns sing out from up and down the line.

The assembled armies of the *kith and kin* charged forward as well.

The clash was epic. Lars reveled in the sounds of shields clanking, swords gutting foes, and bones breaking. Chaos swirled below him as the two groups swept into one another.

There was no line to hold. No palace or city to defend. It was merely two huge assemblies in the deadly dance of war.

He was going to have to remember that line for his memoirs.

A solid *thwack* on his upper shoulder brought Lars' attention back to the field below him.

What the hell? Who had the audacity…

Oh.

That damned troll in her golden helmet stood beneath him.

And she had the gall to grin up at him. It was about all he could see of her face.

"So you gonna just lollygag around all day? Or actually join the battle?" she taunted him.

Lars spewed a stream of acid her direction. It spattered harmlessly down around her, one of those stupid powers of hers keeping her safe.

"I'd planned on letting you watch your entire troop be destroyed before coming to fight you," Lars said. "Letting the loss demoralize you."

Even from the distance he could hear her derisive snort.

"But since you're in such a hurry to die, I may as well accommodate you," he said, flowing down gracefully.

Ah, he was definitely going to have to remember his words, as they'd put that perfect, biting humor for all future demons to behold.

Behold my mighty works, and despair! Or something to that effect.

Lars went to engage not only his enemy, but his future.

DAMN! CHRISTINE HAD BEEN HIDING HOW STRONG her magic had gotten. Lars flew back *again* as her winds knocked him to the side. When had she gotten so skilled? So powerful?

But he saw the flaw in her fighting technique. While her magic was good, her physical form wasn't as strong as he'd first believed. She fought as if she'd only been doing it for a few weeks, not a few years. Heck, she almost threw her ax at him the first time they'd engaged, instead of turning and spinning and striking again, as he'd seen her do before.

Honestly, it had thrown him off. A little.

Her magic had saved her more than once from his most devious attack, that snake-strike-punch he'd worked up just for her, an attack he was certain she wouldn't be able to recover from.

He hadn't even gotten close enough to her to be able to execute the final blow.

Why was she so different? What had he gotten wrong?

In all honesty, if he could withdraw from the battle for a while, he would. Re-review the recordings he'd made of her fighting.

It was almost as if someone else were fighting for her…

Damn it!

Lars rushed forward again, intent on getting close enough to get a good snoutful of her scent. He flew up and over as she jolted him with a lightning attack that Christine had never executed before.

His nose finally told him the truth. That wasn't Christine. Hell, it wasn't even a troll, but a human in troll's armor.

"Who are you?" Lars demanded as he reared back in front of her.

"Took you long enough," came the disdainful reply.

His opponent took off her helmet. Blonde hair came tumbling down.

Tina. The woman he'd tried to marry at one point in order to twist her Destiny. The one that he'd been able to corrupt so thoroughly.

Why hadn't anyone told him that the demonic influence had worn off?

He considered racing toward her again, engulfing her in a series of blows that she'd never be able to defend against. Giving himself at least the satisfaction of her death.

Except…wait. If Tina was here, where the hell was Christine?

"I'll deal with you later," Lars growled at Tina. He turned midair, only to find himself held there firmly.

Tina was a lot stronger magician than she looked.

How could she hold him like this?

He struggled to release himself, freeing first one claw then the next. It was only when he dropped down to the ground that he was able to shake off the spell.

When next he regained the air, he realized that he'd been fooled.

The fight with Tina had been a distraction. He wasn't supposed to see what was going on behind him. He had missed the rest of the battle.

Christine floated above the center of the field, like some stupid Christ figure, with her arms outstretched and light pouring from every pore.

Above her a tall black obelisk rose. Its surface was darkly reflective. Light shone from the top of it, a round mirror that glowed like a miniature sun.

When the light struck the *kith and kin*, the effect was immediate. Either they grew taller, stronger, more fierce, and rejoined the fight with an intensity Lars didn't like.

Or they fled.

Cowards.

But too many of the troops stayed. Far more than Lars would have liked.

While when the light struck the demons…they stood and stared, not moving.

Then, they exploded, their stomachs blowing out.

Not all of them. No, for some, just a part of them caught on fire. Though for a very small portion, nothing at all went wrong.

Lars realized what was happening.

Christine had assembled the obelisk of truth, though he still didn't have a clue what the hell that thing was.

And it was destroying the crystals of corruption, killing those among Lars' troops who'd swallowed them, while merely damaging those who'd carried them.

Fuck.

How was she doing that?

Lars didn't know, but he was going to have to stop her. Now.

CHRISTINE SEEMED TO FEEL HIM APPROACHING, coming out of her trance as he drew near, her ax leaping to her hands.

"Even if you kill me now, you'll still lose," she taunted him. "None of the demons will trust you ever again. You won't be fit to lead a parade, much less an army."

"I will recover from this," Lars swore. "I can. You don't know the plans within plans that I have."

Christine laughed.

She *laughed* at him.

The sound of human laughter still sent Lars into a complete rage. He couldn't help it.

With a mighty roar he flew up to her, his own flaming sword at the ready.

Here was a battle that would be worth all the poetry. Even if it was bad demon poetry.

Lars swung his sword one handed while he kicked out at her at the same time. A double attack that she barely recovered from. If they'd been on the ground, she might have gone down.

Damn it! Lars was going to have to recalculate his plans. Once again.

"You have nothing to fight for," Christine said. "You've already lost. Your troops will turn against you."

"They will follow me!" Lars said. "They will bow down before me! As will all the races of the *kith and kin.*"

"Never," Christine said, striking out with her ax, whirling and aiming her foot at him.

It was a good move, one that he'd seen before. He slashed at her exposed ankle, his claws clanking on the metal that reinforced the calf.

When had she added that to her armor?

Lars struck again and again, but Christine managed to slip away from his sword. He'd still clawed her arms, giving her a scar to remember him by.

If she lived. She wasn't going to live. Was she?

A deep tone sounded above Lars, sounding like the morning bells of a cathedral.

He'd forgotten about the obelisk. It now floated directly above him. Thousands of little white lines squiggled down from it. They didn't touch him, but flickered and waved about three inches above his scales. It looked as though the light was cutting ties flowing out from him.

With sudden horror, he realized that was exactly what it was doing.

All of his demonic influence. All of his corruption spells. All of his conquests.

The light was destroying all the hard work he'd done over the last few years.

Lars *had* to escape before everything was stripped away from him and all he had left was his bare soul.

He glanced at Christine. She knew. She *knew* that this spell would remove all his armor from him, both metaphorically and in the real world.

All that he'd have left would be himself.

For a moment, he saw Christine's soul shine through.

His own soul shrank at the brilliance.

He couldn't take her on his own.

But take her, he would.

Tomorrow.

Lars had insisted on developing the call to retreat. Though his generals didn't like it, and his troops liked it even less. They weren't cowards. They would stay and battle until the very last of them died. Or at least that was what they'd insisted to his face.

Now that Lars' attention was focused below him, he could see that his own army was already breaking apart. Demons were scattering, running for shelter, the troops of the *kith and kin* gleefully dismantling them along the way.

Lars sounded the call to retreat as he dove away,

passing down below Christine who looked a little surprised, but who didn't come after him.

When Lars glanced over his shoulder, he saw that she, too, was caught up in the light of the obelisk.

For a brief moment, he considered returning to attack her.

Except that meant staying in that bare moment.

He shuddered, shaken to his very core.

"Retreat! Retreat!"

Lars watched the huge portals open up across the ground, dirt and ash erupting into the air. Demons went streaming down the great gashes, running for all their might.

He wasn't defeated. The Great War was not over. Not yet.

He could come back from this.

He would not fail again.

CHAPTER THIRTY

Dennis couldn't imagine why Dad had asked him to come to Sunday dinner early. They were all celebrating Christine's latest victory. She hadn't won the war, not yet. There were too many races of the *kith and kin* who had already allied themselves with the demons. And she hadn't been able to kill Lars, though he knew she was finally ready to.

Particularly after the death of Nik.

Dennis didn't have the full story yet, but he knew that his sister blamed herself.

He'd already taken it upon himself to make sure that she got over the war.

This was just one more wound that he was determined to help her heal from.

But now, why Dad?

He'd insisted on meeting Dennis down by the docks instead of inside the house. Then again, Dad had changed so much that summer since coming into his own magic.

He spent a lot of time outside now, even during the blistering heat of July and August.

September was only a few days away.

This year had flown by so fast.

The sky was overcast with a marine layer, the air wet and clammy. It would burn off by midafternoon, the blue sky innocently looking down, as if it had never been covered at all. The stiff breeze off the water carried the smell of musty reeds and reminding Dennis of all the cobwebs gathering in the corners of his living room. He just wasn't home as much anymore.

For some reason, he'd thought he'd have more time off working fulltime for Christine.

Turned out, as he was his own boss now, that he was a much harder taskmaster than any boss he'd ever worked for before.

Who would have thunk it? Him, being more responsible now that he didn't have to report to anyone else?

Fortunately, he still frequently went drinking with various members of the *kith and kin*, so he was still upholding his reputation as a party boy.

For now.

Dad looked miserable, huddled in on himself on a park bench beside the pier, looking out on the water. It wasn't the cold, Dennis could tell that much. It was as if even if the sun did come back out, Dad would never be warm again.

Dennis shook his head. He wasn't given to flights of fancy, not like that.

Hopefully this, too, wasn't a sign of maturity.

"Hey, Dad," Dennis said as he slid onto the solid wooden bench.

"Howdy, Son," Dad said, nodding, but not turning to look at Dennis. "I suppose you're wondering why I asked you to sit with me this morning."

"You okay?" Dennis asked, though he knew the answer from just looking at his dad.

Dad had never looked that old before, not like he did that morning. His skin seemed to reflect the gray pallor of the clouds. Wrinkles had been furrowed around the edges of his face overnight. He even had an old man smell that Dennis had never noticed before.

Weird.

"You'll hear it from the others, but I wanted to make sure you heard it from me, first," Dad said.

Fear struck Dennis' core. "You and Mum aren't getting a divorce, are you?"

Dad laughed. Though it sounded bitter, at least it ended on a more hopeful note.

"No, Son, Lizzie and I are doing fine," Dad said. He cleared his throat. "Mostly."

Dennis nodded. He'd heard from the other *kith and kin* races that always telling the truth seemed to be an aftereffect of standing under the obelisk of truth. At least for a while, as the effect appeared to wear off eventually.

"How long were you at the battle, Dad?" Dennis asked.

"Long enough to get my ass handed to me," Dad replied. He took a deep breath. "You know that some of the beings fled when faced with the truth of their lives?"

"I do," Dennis said. "But no one is shaming them, or

even blaming them. Battles are hard things to face. Particularly if you'd never fought in one before."

Plus, from the tales he'd heard, some of the demons fled the field of battle to go and fight for their loved ones on their own planes.

Their place hadn't been at that battle. They needed to fight someplace else. Or at least that was how Dennis tried to spin the subject every time it had come up.

He was getting good at it, too.

"I fled," Dad admitted.

Dennis nodded. "And it was a damned good thing, too. You know that Christine would never have forgiven herself if you'd gotten yourself killed in her war, right?"

Dad gave another chuckle, softer this time. "That's what she said. And what your mother has said as well."

"Good," Dennis said. "So what's the problem?" It wasn't like Dad to beat around the bush. Sure, he was less blunt than Mum, but that was merely a matter of degree.

"You truly don't mind that I fled?" Dad said.

"You aren't a coward," Dennis said flatly. "None of us think of you that way. And you shouldn't think of yourself that way, either."

"But I left," Dad said, sounding like a much younger, possibly even two-year-old version of his former self.

"And it is much better to leave one battle and survive in order to go fight the next one," Dennis said, trying to put some iron into his voice so that Dad wouldn't try to wiggle out. "We're still proud of you. Hell, I'm still proud of you, and brag on you all the time."

Ah, that seemed to be the key.

It had been Dad's pride that had taken the blow while he'd been protecting his own skin.

"Really?" Dad asked, wonder tinging his tone. "Why?"

"In part, because you're my dad, and you're awesome," Dennis said. It was true. "Even though you're weird and different."

"Son, half our family would be considered pretty weird and different," Dad said, sounding more like his old self.

"But also," Dennis said after a moment, when it appeared that Dad still was waiting for more, "you protected yourself when you needed to most. There are a few who stood and fought even after their hearts told them to go. They mostly died." Dennis shuddered. He'd heard that tale a couple of times. "The few who survived…" Dennis thought for a moment as he tried to put the feeling into words. "They only physically survived. Mentally, I don't know if they'll ever come off that field."

Dad nodded slowly, absorbing the words.

"Your soul told you to leave that battleground. You weren't supposed to be in that place. You did the right thing by going," Dennis said again.

Dad appeared to be taking a few deep breaths, one after another. "You know why I brought you out here? Wanted to meet with you separately? So that you could yell at me, away from the others," Dad said. "I was too much of a coward to let you do that in front of the others."

Dennis rolled his eyes and made sure that Dad saw it. "First off, you're not a coward. You need to stop thinking that way. Next, while I appreciate the opportunity to speak my mind to you privately, I wouldn't have yelled at you in front of everyone else. That's just…rude," Dennis said.

"You didn't always believe that," Dad said quietly.

Dennis couldn't help but roll his eyes again. "Look at me. Growing up and shit. Who would have thought that could happen?"

"Don't be so hard on yourself," Dad admonished.

Dennis merely pointed a finger at him. "Kettle," he said, then he turned the finger around and pointed his finger at himself. "Pot."

"Fine, I take your point," Dad said. "Christine said much the same thing, by the way."

"What, that you weren't a coward? That you did the right thing by leaving?" Dennis said as they both stood up.

"No, that you were growing up into a nice young man," Dad said, the old twinkle returning to his eye. "Dependable. Responsible."

Dennis gave a huge mock shudder. "I'll just have to go out drinking later on tonight to prove her wrong."

Dad laughed and threw his arm over Dennis's neck, giving his shoulder a quick squeeze before letting go.

Dennis swallowed past the lump in his throat. His family used to hug.

Not so much anymore.

At some point, the war would be over, and Dennis could think about dating again.

Though he sometimes wondered if the right girl had already come around once, and he'd missed her.

Naw. He just hadn't found her yet.

Side by side, father and son returned to the rest of the family to celebrate their latest victory.

And to plan for the many more to come.

CHAPTER THIRTY-ONE

CHRISTINE GROWLED LOW IN HER THROAT AS SHE stood beside her dad, watching the cambion carrying demons into the human plane, racing across the fairy bridge. The night was still and quiet around them; the winds had died down, leaving the air chilled. Wet grass curled around her solid boots. Christine pulled the warm red-wool jacket closer around her, trying to keep out the cold.

She hadn't won the Great War. Not yet. She'd won a single great battle. The obelisk of truth had assembled itself when she'd brought the pieces before the army, raising itself and her above the massed soldiers so that all could see.

She'd wondered if there had been a touch of angelic influence at the beginning. It had felt like that, making her uncomfortable in her skin. For a moment, she'd actually thought she'd smelled wood and dust, the scents she frequently associated with Nik.

Then battle had begun and Christine had spent all her energy staying afloat.

She hadn't won the war. Lars and his demons still were coming, were still planning their attacks. Could still come out on top yet.

But how were the cambions crossing the bridge? They were part demon. That made them oath breakers by their very nature.

It wasn't because the human part of them was able to cross. No, if Christine was any judge of demon, these cambion were much more closely aligned to their darker brethren.

A niggling tone sounded under Christine's boots, like a dim bell.

It took Christine a moment to place it.

Though it wasn't exactly the same, it sounded similar enough to the tone that she'd heard once she'd made a promise, when it was recorded under the earth.

"Just a sec," she told her dad. "Keep me safe. Call my name if someone notices us."

"Roger that," Dad said. He pulled out his wand.

Christine had already told him to be careful with that thing. Dad was a much stronger magician than he realized. His strength would have been wasted on the battlefield. He was needed in magical attacks, not physical ones.

But protecting her was something he could do, and it would make him feel better about himself.

Damn this war.

Christine sent her senses down, far under the earth, searching for that dimly ringing bell.

She'd always been told that the promises made by troll

royalty had been written there for any with the skill to read.

Of course, there wasn't actual writing. Her people didn't believe in *books*, a personal failing that she hoped to correct some year.

However, a blazing scene splashed against an empty cavern, deep underground.

Christine felt herself pale as she watched the king give his promise to Manny, the cambion. Her pulse pounded at her temples. Her hands grew clammy. She stiffened her knees so she wouldn't fall down.

Her own people. Her own *king*. Had betrayed her as well as the rest of the *kith and kin*.

The cambion weren't just bringing demons across to the human plane, they were using the fairy bridge as the jumping off point for many worlds and spaces.

And the king had granted them safe passage.

Damn these demons. Damn this war.

Because the only way for the word of troll royalty to be broken was for the troll to die.

Or to be dethroned.

Christine took a gulping breath past the huge lump in her throat.

She couldn't cry. Not now. Not even at this betrayal.

She had yet another war to conduct, with her own people. She could cry rivers of tears afterward.

Determined, Christine rose up above the ground. The orange clouds reflected the streetlights harshly. The stench the demons brought with them rolled over her.

Dad stood tall, strong, and proud beside her. "You okay?" he asked quietly, though he kept most of his attention on the gang of demons in front of them.

Christine nodded rather than trust her voice.

She should go back home. She should make sure her dad got home safely.

However, tonight wasn't a night for safe bets or beds. And her dad needed to prove himself. Not to her, but to himself.

"You wanna help me take them?" she growled as she transformed up, gaining the strength and power of her true troll self.

"Would I!" Dad said, his voice taking on a grim tone that matched how she felt.

"Then let's go play," Christine said, leading the charge.

It was only a dozen demons or so.

And her dad was more than ready.

Leah Cutter writes page-turning fiction in exotic locations, such as a magical New Orleans, the ancient Orient, Hungary, the Oregon coast, rural Kentucky, Seattle, Minneapolis, and many others.

She writes literary, fantasy, mystery, science fiction, and horror fiction. Her short fiction has been published in magazines like *Alfred Hitchcock's Mystery Magazine* and *Talebones*, anthologies like Fiction River, and on the web. Her long fiction has been published both by New York publishers as well as small presses.

Find Leah's books here.

Follow her blog at www.LeahCutter.com.

Reviews

It's true. Reviews help me sell more books. If you've enjoyed this story, please consider leaving a review of it on your favorite site.

Come someplace new...

Are you a traveler? Do you enjoy exploring strange new worlds, new cultures, new people?

Sign up for my newsletter and I'll start you on your travels with a free copy of my book, *The Island Sampler*.

I will never spam you or use your email for nefarious purposes. You can also unsubscribe at any time.

http://www.LeahCutter.com/newsletter/

ABOUT KNOTTED ROAD PRESS

Knotted Road Press fiction specializes in dynamic writing set in mysterious, exotic locations.

Knotted Road Press non-fiction publishes autobiographies, business books, cookbooks, and how-to books with unique voices.

Knotted Road Press creates DRM-free ebooks as well as high-quality print books for readers around the world.

With authors in a variety of genres including literary, poetry, mystery, fantasy, and science fiction, Knotted Road Press has something for everyone.

Knotted Road Press
www.KnottedRoadPress.com